Where Magic Lives

YOLANDE KLEINN

Published by Yolande Kleinn, 2025

www.yolandekleinn.com

Where Magic Lives

By Yolande Kleinn

Book Design: Yolande Kleinn
Cover Art: Kai — https://kindlycrow.carrd.co/
Cover Font: Love Betteria Script from thehungryjpeg.com
Cover Font: Antraste from thehungryjpeg.com
Interior Font: Born from thehungryjpeg.com

First Edition October 2025
Copyright 2025 by Yolande Kleinn

Print ISBN 978-1-946316-63-9
Digital ISBN 978-1-946316-62-2

Chapter One

It must be Nino's magic that calls them, however inadvertently.

Autumn offers an aggressive palette of warm colors all around him, and the weather's been turning so slowly that Nino keeps forgetting to account for the chill when he goes out in the morning. Even today, with the sky a bright and cheerful blue—only the faintest wisp of clouds texturing the southern horizon—the air is so cool that he regrets not bringing a jacket.

His sweater may be soft and cozy and just stylish enough to pass for business casual, but it's not enough to combat the icy wind that sneaks in around him as the evening sun sinks low.

When he cuts through a habitual shortcut between brick buildings, he takes the opportunity to glance around and confirm he's alone. Then, reaching for the magic that lives like a constant hum just beneath his skin, he tugs a little extra warmth out of the air and wraps it around himself. Like a blanket, or a cape, or an especially fond hug. His vision hazes green for a fleeting moment, and he knows if anyone could see him, they would be able to glimpse an unnatural sheen of light swirling all around him, shining brightest in his eyes. But the color fades quickly, and by the time he emerges onto a proper sidewalk again, he's nothing unusual to look at: a gangly man in his thirties with a dark flop of hair, skinny shoulders, and a lopsided smile that rarely leaves his face.

The street he's on now is busier than the one where he disembarked the last bus of his commute. Faces both unknown and familiar pass him by, everyone hurrying along through a crowded rush hour along a hectic sidewalk, pushing their luck at the intersections as car horns honk and traffic crawls forward.

By the time Nino reaches his building, the sky has begun to burnish orange and pink along the uneven skyline—and between some of the buildings, Nino can just make out the colorful glare of sunlight glinting off the river.

He lets his cushion of heat dissipate as he steps into the lobby, the interior space significantly warmer than the outdoors despite the austere minimalism of its design. He shares his elevator ride with several people, but everyone else gets off well before the top floor, and he has an empty hallway to himself for the short final stretch of his journey. It's a relief to step inside the apartment he shares with his best friend, the decor so much softer and more inviting than the public spaces of the building. Arden's boots have been kicked haphazardly into the corner of the little entry hall, but Nino doesn't need this clue to know his roommate is home. Arden's laughter is musical and delighted, echoing through the air and making Nino smile even without knowing what he's laughing at.

The door swings shut, and Nino turns the deadbolt. Slides his own shoes off and sets them deliberately beneath the storage bench. Shrugs the leather strap of his work satchel off his shoulder—then jolts to stillness so sharply he nearly drops the bag from slack fingers. The sensation of magic that skitters across his awareness doesn't feel malicious, but the shock of it sends a rush of ragged air into his lungs. It's faint and unfamiliar, not at all human, and the strangeness trills along his senses.

Wariness twists in the pit of his stomach, and Nino puts his satchel down on the bench before edging toward the living room beyond the tiny entry hall.

Arden's laugh bounces through the air again, and Nino hesitates. Surely there can be no danger here, if his friend sounds like that. True enough, when he finally rounds the corner and peers across the open sprawl of the living room—the overcrowded bookshelves, the oak TV stand, the mismatched green furniture all hazy with the settling sunset—Nino sees nothing amiss. Arden Roy sits on the floor, almost entirely concealed by the couch, nothing but his tousled blond hair visible.

"Is that you, Nino?" Arden calls. A redundant question—it's unlikely any of their friends with a key would let themselves in without knocking first—but Arden sits up straighter, more of his head popping up into Nino's line of sight.

Nino still can't see the bottom half of Arden's face, but he doesn't need to see the man's mouth to know his friend is smiling. He would recognize the deep, delighted crinkles at the corners of those alarmingly blue eyes any day.

"Who else would it be?" And then, despite all the evidence that there is nothing amiss, Nino adds, "Is everything alright?"

Arden's brow furrows. "Of course everything's alright." Then a strange little chirrup whispers through the room, and Arden's head ducks lower again, a snort of amusement escaping him before he says, quietly and clearly not to Nino, "Oh, calm down. Don't be such a diva."

Nino finds himself suddenly certain Arden has done something impossibly foolish like *adopting a dog without consulting him.* Or perhaps a bird. Nino's never heard a dog sound like that, but he could convince himself a cockatiel might.

Then he finishes rounding the couch, and the sight that greets him is such a shock his legs give out beneath him. He lands on his ass with an uncomfortable thump.

Arden looks perfectly normal, if slightly more disheveled than usual, already changed out of the day's suit and jacket in favor of loose jeans and a faded Star Wars t-shirt. But there is nothing normal about the scrawny lizard coiled in Arden's lap, squirming contentedly under the wondering slide of a hand along its back.

That is a dragon. He's never seen one in person, but Nino Casini has studied every book and scroll he's ever been able to get his hands on about magic. He has spent his life asking endless questions of anyone who could hope to answer them. And even now, as terrified disbelief settles into his chest, he feels an equally powerful wonder igniting inside him, lighting his senses and leaving him breathless.

The dragon is definitely an infant, long and slender, and so small its snake-like body would easily fit coiled inside a glove compartment or a lunchbox. It has spindly legs, a frill that circles its narrow head like a mane, a forked tongue that darts out occasionally to scent the air. Iridescent silver scales glint purple in the warm light, and Nino can't tell if this is simply the color of the scales or the shade of the sunset. When the creature blinks, its eyes flash a gold so deep as to look nearly copper, and it takes Nino a moment to realize those eyes are glowing.

When another dragon scurries forward, identical to the first, Nino yelps in surprise. The second creature scrambles clumsily up the front of the couch, tiny claws gripping the velvety material, and then stretches the full length of its body along the arm of the couch. Its little legs splay to either side, and it gives a yawn—so big Nino sees all its tiny, razor-sharp teeth—then flops its head down and closes its eyes.

"What...?" Nino tries very hard to steady out his own breathing, painfully aware that panicking won't do him any favors. "What the hell?"

There are dragons in his home. And Arden Roy—who has no idea magic exists—has found them, and seems utterly charmed by the whole disastrous situation.

"Incredible, aren't they?" Arden's smile is radiant, and when he turns to look directly at Nino, the expression is so overwhelming that it's difficult to keep meeting his eyes. "I found them on the balcony. And it's going to get below freezing tonight. I couldn't leave them outside."

There is something so simple and straightforward in Arden's delight. Nino would not normally describe his best friend as a himbo—the man usually has plenty of cleverness and common sense about him—but today the word seems a remarkably apt description. It's clear he hasn't considered the obvious strangeness of the creature in his lap. From its improbable appearance to the fact that there is no world in which a couple of lizards should have turned up on a twelfth-story balcony... This is ridiculous. It is hopeless and exasperating, and for a moment Nino seriously considers just locking himself in his room and refusing to come out.

That won't accomplish anything, though. So instead he braces himself to sound as natural as he possibly can when he speaks.

"Only you would find a pair of lizards on your balcony and bring them inside instead of calling an animal shelter."

Arden stops petting the creature draped across his ankles and gives Nino a baffled look.

"What?" Nino says, feeling instantly defensive.

"Nino." Arden mutters his name with an achingly familiar rumble of impatience. "They are clearly not normal lizards."

Okay. Maybe Arden isn't so oblivious after all. But Nino can't actually offer up any explanations. Even if he told Arden that yes, these are dragons who should not be anywhere near a metro area, let alone so close to downtown Minneapolis that any number of witnesses might see them... Even if he explained that they should be with a family of older kin, safely away from any human population centers... Even if he theorized about how perhaps two lost infants might follow a deep and innate homing sense to the nearest pull of magic, such as the apartment of a practicing warlock...

He can't explain how he knows any of these things. Not without spilling secrets that aren't Nino's to share.

So he digs his heels into the thinnest pretense and insists, "Who said anything about normal? The world's full of all sorts of strange lizards."

"*Bullshit*," Arden snaps, indignation getting the better of him. His tone startles the dragon on the arm of the couch from its nap, sending it darting away beneath the TV stand. The one on his lap doesn't seem to mind the sharp tone, even when Arden stops petting its head in favor of glowering across the living room.

If there were only one dragon, Nino might stand some chance of convincing Arden the strange scales and glowing eyes are some kind of genetic aberration. But with two of them, identical in every way, right down to the frills crowning their little heads and the long twitching tails, his argument will never land.

Then, even worse, the dragon on Arden's lap unfolds a pair of slender wings from where they've been resting nearly indiscernible along its body. The wings stretch wide, flapping quickly, and the dragon rises into the air to land on Arden's shoulder. The long tail winds behind Arden's neck and then drapes forward down his chest, thumping against the faded logo on his t-shirt.

The dragon breathes a pleased little chirp.

Traitor, Nino thinks.

Arden holds perfectly still while this is happening, clearly startled. But after the dragon settles, he turns his glare once more on Nino, scathing and unimpressed.

Chapter Two

At least Nino manages to convince Arden to keep quiet about the dragons. His actual knowledge isn't much help, since he can't tell Arden anything useful without admitting *how* he knows all these impossible things. But he persuades Arden that their landlord isn't the only reason to keep their unlikely visitors a secret.

Arden was never going to be persuaded by any potential consequences to himself, but when Nino points out the need to keep the dragons safe, he comes around. He agrees to tell no one, and to avoid posting his dozens of photos on social media.

Nino doesn't need to promise to exercise the same restraint. He doesn't have any social media to begin with.

He tries not to worry the next day, as he stumbles his distracted way through a boring job he usually finds completely tolerable. His office walls, colleagues, accounting tasks simply cannot hold his attention. It takes every scrap of willpower just to muddle through the simplest items on his to-do list, rather than checking his phone for crisis texts every five minutes. The fact that Arden is at home to keep the dragons out of trouble doesn't reassure him much. His anxiety grows steadily throughout the day, making him jittery and restless, incapable of staying put at his desk, to the point where multiple coworkers ask if he's feeling okay. It mounts all the way through his afternoon and his long commute home, reaching a fever pitch by the time he steps off the elevator and spots his apartment door at the end of the hall.

The door looks perfectly normal, but Nino can't shake a sense of trepidation. When he turns his key in the lock and the door refuses to swing inward, vindication surges alongside flustered fear.

He pushes harder, and the door budges just a millimeter. Not broken, then. Blocked by something on the other side. He braces his shoulder against the wood and shoves with his full weight, achieving nothing but a faint crunching sound and no give at all.

Something crashes inside the apartment, and Nino's already racing heart picks up the pace as he strives harder with no effect.

"Arden?" he calls, trying to pitch his voice loud enough to be heard inside without alarming anyone in the adjacent apartments—the last thing he needs is to get other people involved—or worse, give anyone reason to think there's an emergency and call the police.

Hard to imagine the police offering productive help in any crisis, but today they would make for a true disaster.

A fire department might be of use. They could at least break down the door for him. But there would still be the problem of the dragons. The potential for discovery. And Nino will only make that call if he has no other options. The fact that Arden isn't answering means it's possible something has gone incredibly wrong. Arden could be hurt. Nino can't fathom how two dragons, so small and helpless and lacking an adult's vast intelligence, might harm a grown man, but he can't shake off the fear.

Another shatter follows a moment later, muffled but alarming, and Nino curses under his breath as he steps back. The woodgrain feels cool and smooth when he sets his palm to the door. Without being able to see what's beyond, his senses are limited, but he focuses his magic forward. Feels out the shape of something wedged against the opposite side of the door, firm and stuck fast.

Then, taking a moment to let raw power coil in his belly—blinking past the sparks of green swirling across his vision in answer to the magic he has called—he draws a slow breath and gives a single, ferocious *push*.

The *something* on the other side of the door gives a resounding crack and the door swings inward. Startled trills meet his efforts, but he can't bring himself to feel guilty for scaring the dragons, whether by dint of the loud noise he just made or the bright surge of his magic. For one thing, this can only be their fault to begin with. For another, Arden might be hurt, and that possibility sends an icy chill through Nino's chest as he pushes his way into the apartment, already searching. He steps carefully, mindful of debris, but drops his work satchel without caring if he damages the laptop inside.

The thing blocking his path was the skinny bookshelf that normally sits directly beside the front door. Not an especially sturdy piece of furniture, really. It must have fallen and wedged just right—probably tipped over beneath the weight of a small climbing lizard—the perfect barricade to bar a door in a small space. It lies across the narrow floor now, splintered almost perfectly in half, its contents of keys and flashlights and phone chargers all scattered in every direction.

Nino closes and locks the door, then hops over the mess and hurries through the apartment calling Arden's name.

His roommate isn't in the living room, but both dragons are. They crouch together on the plush recliner by the window, managing to look so small and guilty that it might be comical if Nino weren't panicking.

Arden isn't anywhere. Not in the kitchen, the bathroom, the laundry nook. Not in either of their bedrooms or the big walk-in closet. There's no sign of him, and while his absence makes the worst of Nino's panic subside, the question of where the hell Arden has gone just makes his head hurt.

The whole apartment is a shambles, other than Nino's room, with its door firmly shut and warded before he left for work this morning. The kitchen is an absolute disaster of things that have clearly been knocked over in a flurry of exploration. Most of the items on the floor aren't actually broken. Metal tins and plastic containers and cutting boards, boxes of energy bars, dishcloths, towels. Every wooden spoon and spatula he and Arden own has ended up on the ground, though the big piece of Red Wing crockery that usually stores them stands sturdy and upright in its place beside the stove.

The box of sodas above the fridge has torn and emptied across the floor, and a couple of the cans have split open and sprayed everywhere. Arden's favorite coffee mug lies in three pieces near the breakfast nook. A couple of glass jars have shattered, and their contents—popcorn kernels and maple sugar, respectively—look like they spilled across the tiles only to be frolicked through by tiny hellions on holiday.

The living room has not fared better. The sturdiest furniture is fine, but multiple picture frames have been knocked off the walls and shattered, leaving glittering shards of glass and a dozen family photos strewn across the rug. One particularly tall bookshelf lies facedown across the middle of the floor, the wood split along one side from impact and all its contents scattered or crushed depending on where they landed. A pair of collectible figurines that usually occupy a small shelf above the television are on the floor. Nino can't tell if they're damaged from where he stands, but something tells him Arden will be spending a lot of money to replace them.

When he looks once more to the culprits on the armchair, he finds they've been watching his appalled circuit of the apartment with enormous gold eyes.

Before Nino can surrender to the useless and ridiculous urge to start lecturing them like disobedient children, he hears the creak of the front door and familiar footsteps, then a click as the door closes.

"What the hell happened?" Arden's voice carries confounded through the otherwise

quiet air, and when he rounds the corner—
shoes still on and careful of where he
steps—he looks surprised to find Nino
already home.

"Your dragons happened," Nino snaps,
his glower burning hotter than necessary to
conceal his shaky relief at the fact that
Arden isn't hurt. "Where did you go? You
were supposed to stay with them."

It wasn't even that big a hardship on
Arden's part. The man is in a truly ludicrous
position financially, between his trust fund
and the cushy management position at his
father's company. It's not like he was going
to get in any trouble for burning a sick day
to babysit a pair of disastrous dragons.

"I was only gone for twenty minutes!"
Arden protests, his handsome face gone a
little bit wild with indignation.

"Why were you gone at all?"

Something more sheepish flickers
across Arden's expression, and he brandishes
one of the bags he's carrying. "They were

hungry. And they like the ethically sourced tuna best."

"Oh my fucking god." Nino squeezes his eyes shut and scrubs a hand across his face, willing himself to calm. Then he blinks and demands, "What's in the other bag?" Both of Arden's burdens are in reusable fabric totes, but the one in his other hand looks significantly heavier than a few cans of tuna.

"Oh. Um. I... also bought us a couple extra fire extinguishers. Just in case," Arden explains. When Nino only blinks at him again, taken completely aback by the absurdity of the situation, Arden mistakes his silence for confusion and adds, "She's not very good at it, but I think one of them is trying to breathe fire. I thought it might be a good idea to plan ahead."

"*She*," Nino echoes helplessly. Not 'it'. God, Arden is already treating them like pets. He stepped out to *buy the dragons a snack*. He bought fire extinguishers just in case.

Nino has the wildly irrational urge to point out that the dragons don't have a gender yet. Not at this early stage, so small they must be practically newborns. But it's so far from being relevant right now, and why should Arden believe him anyway?

Instead, he lets his shoulders slump and says, "Arden, we can't keep them."

"The hell we can't." Arden visibly bristles, his stance and expression turning combative as he straightens up from setting both bags on the floor. Despite his stocky height and broad shoulders, the result is a downright petulant aura, and Nino fights the urge to roll his eyes.

"This building's pet deposit absolutely does not cover fire breathing dragons," he points out reasonably.

"She's only *trying* to breathe fire," Arden retorts. "She's not actually succeeding."

"They'll both figure it out eventually."

"But they're so small!"

"I doubt that will matter when we get arrested for arson." God, it's difficult to refuse Arden when he looks so earnest and insistent—every bit a man accustomed to getting his way—but Nino presses on. "Besides, they won't stay small. They're dragons."

Arden glares indignantly. "How do you know? Maybe they're *tiny* dragons."

He sounds so confident, and Nino has little hope of persuading him. It's not as though he can admit all the things he knows for fact: that dragons can range in scale, from the size of a very small pony to the size of a very large house; that dragons are sentient creatures fully capable of taking care of themselves; that these two infants will eventually grow up and mature into a clever awareness that absolutely disqualifies them as pets.

There is also, unfortunately, the fact that helpless as the little dragons are right now, they would probably get themselves killed in a day if evicted and left to their own devices.

Which means, for all that allowing them to stay is untenable, Nino can't put them out. Not until he figures out what to do with them.

He needs to call his family. Maybe someone else will know what's to be done with a pair of displaced dragon hatchlings in need of care. His aunt Deidre in particular keeps company with more of the magical community than anyone else Nino knows.

Surely if anyone will have useful suggestions to offer, it will be her.

Chapter Three

When Nino was in high school, his sister convinced their parents to adopt a pair of kittens. He vividly remembers the chaos that followed. The shredded upholstery, the chewed-up charging cables, the items knocked off of high shelves. The nonstop noise and mess and dubious wet spots in the carpet, that continued until the little monsters were trained up and settled down enough to actually coexist with humans.

This is so much worse.

Even with Arden alternating between burning his PTO and working from home, Nino locks his bedroom door every time he leaves for work himself. And every day for a week, he comes home to find something else in the apartment has been destroyed. Not by fire, but by tiny claws and tiny teeth and the inevitable fact of gravity, as the little miscreants seem to have a talent for knocking over things that should be sturdy enough to withstand the stress.

Nino doesn't have much of a social life—just a small circle of friends he shares with Arden—but he suspects Arden is beginning to chafe at being confined. Of the two of them, Arden is the one who enjoys going out and meeting new people. He favors overpriced bars where he can flirt with attractive strangers of any gender or persuasion. He must surely be struggling with the solitude required by keeping this new secret.

On Saturday, when Nino volunteers to stay alone with the dragons so Arden can finally go out for a few hours, Arden gives him a look so dubious it's almost insulting.

"Oh my god, don't look at me like that." Nino rolls his eyes. "I'm not going to sneak them out of the apartment while you're gone."

"You have spent the entire week trying to convince me they can't stay."

"They can't," Nino insists mulishly. "But I'm not going to just make them disappear when you're not looking. They clearly can't take care of themselves. I'm not a complete monster."

Arden considers him wordlessly for a long moment before striding across the kitchen to stand directly in front of Nino. He is suddenly too close, and his proximity sets off an unaccountable flutter in Nino's chest. Arden's gaze catches and holds Nino's own, steady and inescapable.

"You promise they'll still be here when I get back?" Arden asks.

Nino squashes down his affront, consciously choosing not to be offended by Arden's skepticism. Nino *has* been arguing all week for getting rid of the dragons, even while struggling with the matched quandaries of having no idea where to take them and not knowing how to explain his knowledge once he manages to acquire it. Aunt Deidre promised to put out the query on his behalf, but even if she eventually calls Nino back with a solution to the problem, there will remain the conundrum of how to convince Arden without admitting things that have every chance of damaging their friendship beyond repair—secrets that are not Nino's alone to divulge.

Finally, putting a decade of affection and all his sincerity into the answer, Nino says softly, "I promise. I wouldn't do that to you."

The hand Arden sets to his arm a moment later feels too heavy, and Nino wonders how a touch can feel so intensely meaningful when he has no idea what it means. Still, Arden's expression is clearing, and a smile twitches at one corner of his unreasonably pretty mouth.

Only after Arden is gone and Nino has the whole apartment to himself, does he gather both dragons into his lap to try something he probably should've attempted days ago.

It isn't an especially precise spell. A more studied warlock than Nino would probably be able to bring more exactitude to the endeavor, and less clumsy intention. But Nino has only ever had his instincts and his patchwork of reading to guide him when it comes to magic. He wouldn't have known to attempt this if his aunt hadn't suggested it, and he can only do his best. So he allows inexpert earnestness to shape the spell, one hand resting on each dragon—their scales disconcertingly smooth against his palms— as his vision goes hazy and bright.

The dragons blink up at him through the rush of green, clearly not alarmed by the intrusive magic fluttering along their scales and slipping beneath their skin. One of them even wriggles harder into the press of Nino's hand as though asking to be petted, but Nino doesn't oblige. He keeps his focus on the search he is weaving through them, a call that finds what it's looking for within the little dragons and then reaches outward—past the walls of the apartment and farther, farther, farther—searching for a likeness elsewhere, as far as he can extend himself.

The new awareness of his surroundings is so strange and expansive that it's difficult to keep everything in his head at once. So much life, not just in this building but on the street below, the river nearby, the parks and pathways and suburbs beyond. He can feel the quieter sprawl of more rural towns and the spaces between them.

He's never done anything quite like this. If he had guessed before the attempt, he would've hoped to extend his senses to encompass the metro area, perhaps some of the suburbs surrounding the Cities. He's shocked to have almost the whole of Minnesota humming along his awareness, right there at his fingertips. Wide open to his perusal.

And what he's searching for simply is not here.

He lets the magic fade and peers down at the guileless gold of two pairs of slitted eyes peering up at him. A pang of protectiveness and grief slips between his ribs, and he finally lets his palm slide along the wriggling dragon's back in a soothing caress.

"What happened?" Nino asks softly, even though they probably don't know and couldn't answer if they did. Even older and wiser dragons don't use human language.

Wherever their family went, it would have to be hundreds of miles away for Nino's search to fail so spectacularly at finding them. And no adult dragon would ever willingly abandon an infant. He'll never know for certain how these two ended up alone in the city, but he would gamble his entire life savings on the awful certainty that their guardians are dead.

Both dragons wriggle on his lap now, restless perhaps because they sense Nino's quiet heartache, even if they're too young to understand what it means.

"I'm so sorry," he murmurs, wishing he could do anything at all to make this right.

He traces gentle fingers across their necks and backs, and prays his aunt can help him keep the little hellions safe.

*

The apartment is less of a disaster than usual the next evening, when Nino comes home from work to Arden's proud announcement that he has finally chosen the perfect names for their small, destructive guests.

"Arden, no." Incredulity shapes the syllables, and Nino stands perfectly still at the edge of the living room. He's just about as far as he can possibly be from the door to the kitchen, where his confoundingly stubborn roommate stands wiping both hands on a towel. The smell of Nino's favorite stir-fry wafts through the apartment and makes his stomach growl, but this blatant attempt at bribery isn't enough of a distraction to prevent him from making his point. "They're dragons. You can't name them. We're not keeping them."

"Shows what you know," Arden retorts cheerfully. He tosses the towel on the counter behind him and crosses his arms over his chest, a careless pose that calls Nino's attention inexorably to his muscular forearms. "Not only *can* I name them, but I already did, and their names are perfect. Thematic masterpieces. And obviously we're keeping them. Dragons are amazing."

Nino mumbles a whole string of words his mother wouldn't approve of, squeezing his eyes shut and pinching the bridge of his nose. The first faint throb of a headache won't be dispelled though. He tries to simply ignore the irritation, and opens his eyes to glare at Arden.

"I'm not conceding any of those points." He sets his satchel on the floor—better the floor than on top of a piece of furniture where it has farther to fall if a tiny winged reptile knocks it down. "But fine, what are their names?"

It feels like such a ridiculous question to ask about a pair of dragons who are too young to understand language, and who look literally identical. Even now, glancing across the living room, Nino can't tell which one is which. One dragon is curled on the soft rug in the middle of the room, looking peaceable enough except for the way she seems to be contorting her little body and puffing billows of smoke in an attempt to ignite the material beneath her. The other is stretched along the top edge of the flat-screen television, looking remarkably comfortable in what should be a precarious position, watching everything with wide eyes.

Arden just grins as though Nino has conceded defeat, and explains. "Toast is the one who keeps trying to set things on fire. And Pigeon is... well... she's not very bright."

Irritation flares hotter in Nino's chest, so many frustrations coalescing inside him at once, and suddenly it takes far more effort than it should not to snatch up the nearest un-shredded pillow and hurl it at Arden's head.

"First of all, pigeons are incredibly intelligent. It's not their fault that they're bad at building nests in unsuitable environments, and it's even less their fault that humans domesticated them and then abandoned them to fend for themselves." Nino knows that nothing Arden has said truly warrants this snappish tone, and yet he can't seem to modulate his voice as he continues, "Second of all, how do you know she's not very bright? Maybe she's just shy."

He can't fathom why he is arguing this point, or why he cares. Bright or not, why should he give a single fuck what kind of dragon she is? Neither dragon is going to stay. Nino will be the goddamn adult in this situation, because one of them needs to do it, and clearly it won't be Arden. Then again, when is it ever Arden? The man is rich and spoiled and accustomed to getting what he wants. Arden Roy rarely needs to worry about complications or consequences, with his stupid trust fund and his pretty face. Yes, he's sweet and agonizingly sincere, but he's also *ridiculous*, and Nino should not feel this protective of him.

Nino shouldn't have to stand alone in handling the situation like a rational adult.

But even now, he can tell from the mischievous glint in Arden's eyes that this discussion isn't over.

Just as Arden opens his mouth to argue, the dragon on top of the television—Pigeon, Nino concedes, because it actually is alarmingly easy to tell which is which despite their identical features—topples from her perch. She doesn't fall far, landing on top of the massive TV stand with a flutter, right next to the current gen gaming console that has miraculously survived the week unscathed. She quickly scrambles to her feet, then stands there blinking rapidly and looking disoriented, staring up at the top of the television like it somehow betrayed her.

"Look in her eyes, Nino." Laughter rumbles in Arden's voice. "There's *nothing there*. No thoughts at all. She's got no idea what's going on around her."

"Oh, and the one who keeps trying to commit arson has?"

"Yes." Arden's smile spreads, sly and confident. "I'll show you."

"This'll be good." Nino rolls his eyes.

"Toast, *no*," Arden says, interrupting the dragon on the floor in the process of coiling up her body for another incendiary attempt. His tone comes out the firm command of a dog trainer, and Nino is shocked to see the little menace uncoil obediently and peer up at Arden. A moment later, Arden murmurs more gently, "Toast, come here."

Nino watches in disbelief as Toast obeys the command. Rather than opening up her wings and flying the distance across the room, she scuttles—adorable and lizard-like—along the floor. When she reaches the door to the kitchen, she catches her little claws in Arden's pant leg and climbs deftly up the outer seam of his jeans. When she nears his waist, Arden lowers a hand and lets her coil along his palm and wrist so he can set her on his shoulder.

Nino scowls and refuses to find the demonstration charming.

"See?" Arden looks sunny and pleased, and he scritches the dragon beneath her narrow jaw. Toast chirps and wriggles into the touch, then burrows comfortably into the crook of Arden's shoulder as he turns his focus to the other dragon.

"Pigeon," Arden says. The dragon beside the television lifts her head, long neck arching curiously as she regards Arden with those huge eyes. Clearly recognizing the sound of her name, much to Nino's chagrin, but otherwise having no idea how to respond. After a moment, Arden says in the exact same tone he used to call the other dragon, "Pigeon, come here."

Instead of obeying, Pigeon gives an ecstatic little trill, and a squirming hop that knocks over the gaming console. A stack of games and other discs topple toward the floor with it, and all of this sudden chaos sends her careening into the air on a frantic flutter of wings.

Nino barely resists the urge to magically soften the console's landing. Focused as he is on fending off an impulse so instinctual, he nearly falls over at an unexpected weight on his shoulder. He turns his head so fast his neck twinges, only to discover that Pigeon has flown straight for him, landing clumsily and clinging to Nino's jacket with tiny claws that are sure to leave punctures in the leather.

It does not escape his notice that Pigeon has not even come close to obeying the spoken command. Instead of flying to Arden, she has inadvertently landed as far away as possible while still remaining in the living room.

Arden arches one eyebrow, an *I told you so* that does not require a single spoken word. Nino glares at his smug and lovely face for a moment, then glares down at Pigeon, who has climbed the rest of the way up and looped herself loosely around Nino's neck. She's peering up at him, her frontmost claws latched uncomfortably into his shoulder. Her eyes are still wide, but they offer him a slow blink, and he silently concedes that Arden is probably right about her comparative intelligence.

Nino hates it when Arden is right about things.

"I'm not picking all that up." He nods at the new mess on the floor—the console surrounded by discs and cases and a thoroughly demolished organizational system. As far as he's concerned, Arden had a direct hand in creating the mess. That makes it his disaster to sort out.

When Nino turns to collect his work satchel and storm into his own room, Pigeon is still coiled loosely around his neck like a scarf, and he makes no effort to put her down.

Chapter Four

It's a good thing Arden has an unreasonable amount of money, as one week turns into a month with two tiny, destructive dragons underfoot.

Nino has been repeatedly in touch with his aunt, who keeps promising that the search for a safe solution continues. None of Deidre's personal friends and contacts have offered up the answers Nino needs, but everyone who's been in touch has further connections of their own to explore. Which means Nino has no choice but to be patient and wait as this quiet, secretive network of magical folks reaches out and out in an ongoing search.

Toast and Pigeon have managed to do a truly alarming amount of damage in the meantime, despite the fact that they haven't grown at all in such a short span. This, despite Toast's continuing failure to set anything on fire. Between claws, teeth, and clumsy flight, nearly every piece of furniture in the living room has needed replacing—some more than once—not to mention anything more breakable. The gaming console meets its demise not long after miraculously surviving its first fall, and the television topples and cracks two days after that.

It's frankly a wonder no one has filed a noise complaint. Between heavy items dropping at unpredictable intervals, and the way Arden gleefully roughhouses with Toast like the little dragon is an energetic puppy, Nino is just about ready to go out of his mind from the noise. Chalk one up for the sound-reduction in the floors of these fancy apartments.

The destruction barely diminishes when Arden buys the dragons a massive and complicated cat tower, but Nino can admit through his incredulity that the results are adorable. There is something endearing about coming home to find a dragon curled up asleep inside a small fabric-lined cubby at eye level.

Not that Nino has any intention of admitting this to his shameless and delighted roommate.

At least Arden's been able to keep working from home, ensuring the dragons are never alone in the apartment. It's exhausting and frankly unsustainable—just one more reality Arden is stubbornly ignoring in favor of his delusions that they will be able to keep their new guests forever—and even more so when simple household chores are factored into the equation. Nino is not accustomed to doing chores with his hands. That's what magic is for. But unless he wants Arden to catch him in the kitchen with dirty dishes washing themselves while the vacuum runs in the study and the laundry folds itself...

Nino's been stuck managing it all the normal way for weeks, and he hates every moment.

A sullen, rational corner of his mind recognizes that he agreed to this. He pays almost no rent at all, because this is the balance they struck when Nino first moved in. But he still can't stand having to do everything the hard way, when he is so accustomed to the process being effortless.

Occasionally Arden goes away long enough on the weekends that Nino can use his magic for a while. Nino takes these opportunities to manage as many chores as he can, and to shore up the walls and furniture against inevitable destruction. He does his best to ignore the way Pigeon and Toast follow him around while he manages these tasks, clearly fascinated by his magic. He hopes they aren't imprinting on him like baby ducklings. The last thing he needs is for a pair of lost dragons to think he's their mom.

The other problem with Arden being home all the time is more personal. Suddenly Nino finds himself living more in his roommate's pocket than ever—their usual closeness distorting and shifting with this near-constant contact—setting off confusing new sensations in Nino's chest when he least expects. Surely they should be sick of each other by now, desperate for what time apart they can manage. Instead, Nino finds himself drifting into Arden's orbit in whole new, disorienting ways. Craving his company and enjoying the new secret they share—wondering with fleeting recklessness what it might be like to share other secrets.

What would it be like, to tell Arden about his magic? To stop hiding this fundamental piece of himself from his best friend?

The night Nino falls asleep watching a movie on their replacement television, he doesn't actually intend to drift off. It's just been such a long day, overtime at work thanks to a looming deadline, and he'll need to get up early tomorrow to finish the project. When his mind eventually fumbles back to wakefulness, he's lying across the couch with his head in Arden's lap and a dragon curled contentedly on his chest. The dragon—almost certainly Pigeon considering how she favors Nino—is breathing in *whuffing* little snores. And Arden...

Arden's fingers are carding through Nino's hair, fingertips tracing idle patterns along his scalp, and it feels so good he pretends he's still asleep.

They don't talk about it, even after Nino finally acknowledges that he's awake and they part ways for the night. He doesn't know what to make of the way Arden watches him the next morning, sidelong and cagey, averting his eyes whenever Nino catches him looking. It's unnerving, and even once they've regained their equilibrium a couple days later—navigating around each other in the closest they ever come these days to a normal Saturday—Nino doesn't know what to do with the warmth in his chest, familiar and strange all at once.

When someone knocks on their door that afternoon, Nino has all of two seconds to be glad for the distraction before better sense reminds him just how disastrous it would be to let anyone into the apartment right now. Even worse, there are only a couple of people who can make it all the way to their door rather than needing to be collected from the lobby, when even the elevators require an electronic key fob to function. No one has called out *Maintenance!* through the door, which means it's one of Arden's or Nino's closest friends, arriving unannounced, probably worried over their conspicuous absence from a month's worth of social events.

Nino glances toward the kitchen and finds Arden staring at him, a panicky expression on his face, Toast perched precariously on his head. The quiet feels suddenly oppressive, but Nino holds his finger to his lips. Urging silence. Unnecessary, judging by how very still Arden is standing.

Pretending they're not home is the only way to get whoever's at the door to leave without coming inside.

It seems like a perfectly good plan, right up until the moment a loud crash accompanies the sight of the television—the *new television*, rest in peace—clattering to the floor, Pigeon standing startled in the space that would have been concealed behind it a moment ago.

"*Fuck*," Nino growls, turning toward the front hall just in time to hear the door unlock—the click and creak as it opens and slams shut—the rush of footsteps, and then a stocky woman with dark skin appearing around the corner. Ishiko looks frantic and

worried, but otherwise as lovely and
fashionable as ever in a deep blue peacoat.
Nino's heart is racing, trepidation alight
beneath his skin, but he's also relieved
Ishiko is the one standing here surveying
the situation. Of all their mutual friends,
she's the one with the most level head.

And more importantly, she can keep a
secret.

"Are you both okay? What—" Ishiko
stares down at the fallen television, then up
at Pigeon as her eyes go comically wide,
looking even bigger for the dark eyeliner
and mascara she favors. "What the hell is
that?"

Pigeon responds by skittering down into
the narrow space behind the now-empty TV
stand, completely out of sight. Ishiko stares
at the spot for a disbelieving moment, then
glances at Nino. He offers what he hopes is a
reassuring smile, but it must fall badly short
because her stare skates immediately away
and finds Arden instead. She does a double
take at the sight of Toast perched on Arden's

head, her expression blinking with the kind of intense focus that suggests she's trying to sort out if she's hallucinating.

Then she turns and glares at Nino—as though any of this is his fault—and demands in a voice that will not be denied, "Explain."

"Um." Nino worries his lower lip between his teeth for a moment, weighing imperfect options. "Okay. Would you... like to sit?"

Ishiko continues to glare at him, but she nods, then shrugs out of her coat before plopping herself down at the center of the big couch. She tucks both legs up onto the cushion with her, sitting cross-legged and clasping her hands expectantly in her lap. At least she's glancing back and forth between them, rather than glowering like Nino is somehow to blame for this mess. Her expression looks a little less furious now that her fear for their wellbeing is fading, but her mouth is still twisted into a glower.

Nino lets himself turn away from her, ignoring the fallen television and moving to peer as best he can behind the TV stand.

"Hey," he says softly, drawing Pigeon's squirrely attention. "It's all right. You can come out."

She doesn't, of course. It's not as though she has any idea what he's saying, unlike her sister. But she visibly relaxes at his tone. And when he holds out a hand, she finally squeezes free of her hiding place and wriggles up his arm, clinging to his sleeve with her claws and blinking huge eyes.

"Oh my god," Ishiko breathes. She's watching him when he turns around, but glances to her left when Arden and Toast sit down beside her on the couch.

Toast, ever the fearless little adventurer, scurries down from Arden's head, then climbs across his shoulder and arm, to drape herself across Ishiko's denim-clad thigh. The little frill around Toast's head gives a happy twitch, and while Toast's mouth isn't exactly equipped for such human expressions as smiling, the way she blinks those enormous eyes up at Ishiko exudes unmistakable delight.

"I think she likes you," Arden announces brightly, in a tone that is clearly designed to try and make this situation seem normal by force of will.

"Can I?" Ishiko asks, hand hovering above the dragon's head without quite touching.

"Oh, certainly." Arden grins. "Toast loves attention."

"*Toast?*" Ishiko laughs. She traces her fingers reverently along the smooth scales of the dragon's forehead, then follows a longer path along the graceful neck.

"And that one's named Pigeon," Arden adds, throwing Nino a pleased look.

Nino rolls his eyes and claims the other side of the couch, humans and dragons bookending their unexpected guest. He wonders if he can convince Pigeon to sit in Ishiko's lap too. She looks so smitten with Toast, her gaze soft and awed and warm.

But as soon as Nino lifts his arm to make the attempt, Pigeon squeaks in alarm, wriggling the rest of the way up his arm and down the back of his shirt. She squirms under the turtleneck of his sweater so quickly that Nino couldn't intercept her if he tried.

"Hey!" he squawks, reaching uselessly as Pigeon's wriggly little body curls at the small of his back.

Arden's laughter is bright and booming, and it brings an inexplicable blush to Nino's cheeks as he glares back and forth between Arden and Ishiko. Ishiko's expression is one of barely restrained mirth, as though she is trying very hard not to laugh for fear of offending Nino; Arden's is wide open and so full of amusement that Nino blushes harder, even though he has no reason to be so startled at the bright, intense blue of Arden's eyes.

"You'll have to forgive Pigeon," Arden says more softly a moment later. "She's shy."

"Clearly." Humor brightens the warm alto of Ishiko's voice. Any last vestiges of worry and anger are gone now, and she continues to pet Toast as she glances between Nino and Arden. "I assume this is why you've both fallen off the face of the planet these past few weeks."

"Is that why you're here? Were you worried about us?" Arden teases, nudging her with a shoulder—the show of affection has absolutely no business making Nino feel jealous, and he bites his cheek to keep his mouth shut—wonders if he can blame the dragons for this too.

"Of course I was worried." Ishiko makes no effort to conceal her exasperation as she sets a hand to Arden's shoulder and pushes back. "It's not like either one of you to go completely radio silent. We wondered if you'd both been kidnapped, or maybe eloped without telling us."

Nino's eyes widen, his pulse picking up all over again for no goddamn reason, but Arden just snorts and says, "First of all, who on earth would kidnap *Nino?* And second, you can't honestly think we'd elope instead of having a great big party where people are required to get us presents and say nice things about us."

"Mmm," Ishiko hums agreeably. "Well. I'm very glad you're both okay. Now are you going to tell me what the hell is going on?" She arches one eyebrow and nods down toward the dragon on her lap, and Nino realizes there's no point keeping her in the dark at this point. Ishiko won't believe Pigeon and Toast are normal lizards any more than Arden did.

So Nino and Arden explain. It's a bit garbled, a bit meandering, but between them they manage to cover the necessary ground. Nino makes no mention of his own magic— if he can't tell Arden, he sure as hell can't tell anyone else—but otherwise he holds nothing back.

By the time there's nothing left to tell, Toast has fallen fully asleep in Ishiko's lap. Pigeon has crawled out from beneath Nino's sweater to coil loosely around his knee, allowing Ishiko to pet her little head.

"We're going to find them somewhere safe to go," Nino says, watching Pigeon's expression turn sleepy and blissed out, like a contented cat.

"No." Arden reaches over to stroke a thumb across Toast's back. "We are keeping them forever."

Nino glares at him, and Arden smiles back. In the space between their stalemate, Ishiko laughs and is no help at all.

Chapter Five

When he finally gets the call he's been waiting for—his aunt's name across the screen of his phone and some *actual answers* from the woman's network of magical acquaintances—Nino's heart does too many things at once. Amid the onslaught of contending emotions, he can't decide which is the most powerful. Relief, that he will finally be able to do right by these dragons and get them out of his home? Fear, at the prospect of convincing Arden without giving away Nino's most closely guarded secrets?

Maybe what he feels most powerfully is disappointment at the prospect of saying goodbye. He tried so hard not to get attached. He probably shouldn't be surprised at how spectacularly he failed.

A rescue sanctuary for orphaned dragons sounds like the perfect solution to an impossible quandary, and Aunt Deidre insists one of her closest friends will vouch for the care the dragons will receive. Once Pigeon and Toast are a little older, they'll be strong enough and clever enough to exist in the world exactly as they are. When Nino asks why such a trusted friend took so long giving her an answer, Deidre huffs an irritated sound and points out that not everyone likes being easy to contact. Magic users have even more motivation—and ability—to live off the grid than most people, and perhaps Nino shouldn't be so judgmental.

Nino grudgingly acknowledges the point. He's got depressingly few magical acquaintances himself, living as he does in a city that requires him to be constantly hiding his talents. If someone didn't have Nino's phone number, they would be hard-pressed to contact him too.

He puts off telling Arden anything that night, rationalizing that he needs a solid strategy and irrefutable arguments first. Tomorrow will be soon enough to have the difficult conversation.

As Nino settles beneath his covers for sleep, he pushes away a faint twitch of guilt at postponing the inevitable. He tugs his curtains shut with his hands instead of using magic, since the window is right there within reach, taking up most of the wall alongside his bed. His pillows are soft and inviting after a long day, and he burrows into them with a tired sigh. Near his feet, he feels the barest dip of the mattress and then the light pressure of Pigeon coiling over his ankles on top of the blankets. No surprise there. He didn't close his bedroom door fast enough to keep out a dragon, and this has become Pigeon's habitual sleeping spot.

Toast has taken to sleeping in Arden's room just as reliably, and Nino wonders in a sleepy and idle sort of way if it's anything like this. Arden's bed is significantly larger than Nino's. Maybe Toast sleeps on one of the spare pillows, huffing and snoring and occasionally trying to set Arden's hair on fire.

The image makes Nino smile, even as thoughts of Toast's increasingly frequent arson attempts bring him back to the unpleasant inevitability of making the dragons someone else's problem. How is he supposed to persuade Arden of the necessity for this? How can he convince his best friend the dragons will be safe, when Nino is not supposed to understand any more about magic than Arden is? How will he explain knowing about the sanctuary in the first place?

For about ten seconds, he considers the possibility of transporting the dragons there without telling Arden, but it simply isn't feasible. The sanctuary is a significant distance away, right on the border between Ontario and Manitoba. Twelve hours by car. Less time but more numerous complications by plane. Neither option is anything like workable.

Arden is the one who owns a car, and Nino wouldn't know how to drive it even if he wanted to borrow the vehicle without permission. Even if he trusted himself to safely make the long trip alone, with two destructive and energetic dragons in the backseat. He can't bribe Ishiko for a ride, either. She would demand to know why Arden isn't involved and then probably refuse to help him. And when he tries to picture packing the dragons up into cat carriers and taking them through airport security, he nearly tumbles back to full wakefulness at the sheer absurdity of the image.

And honestly, more important than any of these complications is the simple fact that—even if he could pull it off—Arden would be heartbroken to lose the dragons without saying goodbye.

He'll be heartbroken to lose the dragons in any case. Nino knows this with a soft, sad certainty that he stubbornly refuses to let transform into guilt. Pigeon and Toast have wormed their way into Arden's heart. He's going to be devastated to lose them, even if Nino manages to convince him this is the right thing to do.

So the conversation will wait until tomorrow. And as Nino drifts off to the quiet rhythm of Pigeon breathing at the foot of the bed, he tries without success to figure out what he can possibly say.

He wakes disoriented and startled, not sure of the time but very confident there shouldn't be light reaching him through his closed eyelids. It can't be dawn yet—not when his eyes feel so gritty and his limbs are still heavy with sleep—and he shouldn't be this uncomfortably warm beneath the blankets, when he's wearing only a pair of boxers and a t-shirt. A second later he registers a wriggling weight on his chest, tiny claws pawing at him more urgently by the second. When a sharper sting catches him, breaking the skin, Nino opens his eyes and startles upright so suddenly that Pigeon rolls down into his lap.

His eyes dart, instant and horrified, to the glow near the foot of the bed. For several seconds he watches in frozen disbelief as flames spread up from the bottom of the curtain with dizzying speed.

The fire dances too close to his feet, and Nino jolts from his stupor with a cry of alarm, jerking away from the painful heat. He yelps an even less dignified sound when the momentum tips him over the edge of the mattress. He bangs his wrist painfully on his bedside table as he lands with bruising force on the hard floor. His ass and elbow take the brunt of the impact, and Nino feels a tingle rush along his arm from smacking his funny bone in exactly the wrong way. He's already bracing his hands behind him, scuttling backward in a clumsy rush.

Pigeon follows him, eyes wild and frantic, wings fluttering through the air. She lands in her habitual loose coil around Nino's neck, tail thumping anxiously against his chest.

A perplexed corner of Nino's mind wonders at the smoke detector failing to react to the spreading fire, and only now does he register that the flames are the wrong color. Deep indigo and even deeper purple cascade into a sharp, sheening silver. Darting tongues of flame lick their way up the curtains and catch the bedclothes. There's no smoke at all—only this unnatural brightness and heat—spreading far too quickly, igniting everything it touches.

Nino has never seen dragon fire before, but there's no mistaking it now that it's right here before his eyes. A panicked rasp of laughter claws from his chest. He has spent weeks anxiously watching Toast try to set things on fire—only for Pigeon to be the one who succeeds, inadvertently and probably in her sleep.

Before Nino figures out how to react to this unlikely fiasco, Arden bursts through the door in a sleepy stumble. He's wearing a pair of loose sweatpants and nothing else. Toast clings owlishly to his sleep-disheveled hair.

"Are you okay?" Arden rubs a hand across his eyes and stifles a yawn. "I thought I heard— What the *fuck*?" His eyes widen, his whole demeanor instantly alert as he takes in the spreading inferno.

"I'm okay," Nino says from his place on the floor, his own attention snapping back to the flames. His magic rises instinctively in answer, twisting through Nino's chest, burnishing the edges of his vision with a reassuring green glow. He moves without conscious thought, raising a hand toward the conflagration. He holds his palm out toward the bonfire that used to be his bed and lets the irresistible magic hurtle through him.

The reckless rush of power shocks along his senses, glinting so brightly across his vision that for several seconds he can't see past the glow surrounding his body, the shine filling his eyes.

But he doesn't need to see. He can feel the contours of the fire, and he lets his magic surround it. Contain it. Then finally twist the fire right out of existence, just as what's left of his bed frame collapses with a resounding crack.

Chapter Six

Nino's ass and elbow ache spectacularly as Arden helps him to his feet, but these pains are nothing compared to the delayed panic squeezing tight around his heart.

His secret is out. He used magic in front of Arden. Now his best friend won't meet his eyes, and Nino's legs are shaking so hard he can barely stand.

He follows Arden out of his bedroom, studying the tense set of bare shoulders, the unaccustomed tightness of Arden's clenched jaw. Pigeon stirs where she's draped behind Nino's neck, her nose snuffling into the crook of his shoulder and her tail thumping restlessly. The sky beyond the glass balcony windows is dark, though light pollution illuminates low-hanging clouds. In the center of the living room, Arden stands perfectly still, looking smaller than he should. Lost. Shaken. His expression is closed-off and unreadable as he reaches up to pluck Toast off his head and hold her in his arms, where she promptly drowses back to sleep.

Coward that Nino is, it's Arden who speaks first. "You used magic to put out the fire."

He sounds detached and wrong. But when Nino whispers his name, soft and pleading—when Arden turns and finally looks at him—there is wounded rage in the usually soft blue of his eyes.

"Have you always...?" Arden starts, voice deeper than usual, roughened by unaccustomed gravel. "Did you already know...?" He can't seem to finish the question. He probably doesn't know the right words, or maybe he's still struggling to wrap his head around what he saw Nino do. The shift in his reality must be staggering, even after a month of knowing dragons are real.

"Yes," Nino says, sparing him the effort of finding the right way to frame an impossible question. "I've always been able to do things like this."

"*Why didn't you tell me?*" The words come out so harsh that Toast startles awake in Arden's arms and scrambles halfway up his chest, claws digging into his skin and making him flinch. He plucks her back into a less painful hold, shaking his head as though to dislodge unpleasant thoughts. There's a first sheen of moisture glittering in Arden's eyes, though his expression has settled into anger rather than heartbreak.

"Arden, I *couldn't* tell you." Nino's vision blurs, and he tilts his head back, staring up at the dim ceiling and blinking hard. He's not going to cry, no matter how viciously the panic of discovery is coursing through his body. This is too important. His heart races, and his whole chest clenches. He is terrified of saying the wrong thing, of taking Arden's display of hurt and outrage and answering it so badly he loses his best friend.

When he manages to look directly at Arden again, he finds a more guarded expression waiting for him.

"So you're... what?" Arden says. "Some kind of sorcerer?"

"Warlock is... really the, um... technical term." Nino grimaces the instant the words are out of his mouth, even before Arden's eyes widen with angry disbelief.

"There's a *technical term* for something like this?"

Nino could try to explain. About the strange, scattered contours of the world of magic hidden at the edges of the world Arden knows. About the winding history of magic, well documented but difficult to access, and Nino Casini's own limited interactions with those resources. About his family and the things they can do. About the community Nino has so little contact with, because he chooses to live in the city with Arden.

It's not that he's chosen his best friend over a more magical community on purpose. It's just that, since meeting Arden, he's never quite convinced himself to leave.

The breath that fills Nino's lungs feels unsteady, and his voice isn't much better when he finally says, "I'm sorry." He makes himself continue despite the way Arden's eyes narrow. "I didn't want to lie to you. But when you spend your whole life hiding who you are, it's not like you can just pick and choose when to stop."

"We've been friends for ten years."

"Yes." Nino stares at Arden, willing him to understand. To forgive Nino for what must surely feel like the most personal betrayal, especially to a man as unreservedly honest as Arden Roy.

"*Ten years*, Nino," Arden repeats, incredulous.

"I fantasized a hundred times about telling you. Showing you. I always imagined

I would come clean one day, and I'd find just the right way to broach the subject so you wouldn't hate me." Doing so would break the trust of everyone who relies on him to guard these secrets—his family and the rest of the magical world—but Nino's words are sincere. It was only a matter of time before his sense of duty crumbled in the face of his affection for Arden. Even now, if the truth hadn't come out, Nino's hesitation would probably stem more from fear of losing his friend than from responsibility to anyone else.

Arden's scowl deepens, and Nino flinches, not sure how this speech can possibly have made the situation worse.

Then Arden jerks his gaze away, out past the window without seeming to take in the horizon beyond. "Did you really think I would hate you?"

Nino straightens with a jolt. "Arden—"

But even if he could somehow conjure up the right words to fix this, he doesn't get the chance. Arden is already moving, dropping Toast gently on the couch as he strides past and disappears into his own bedroom with a slam of the door. Nino stands frozen at the center of the living room, blinking at the closed door until it opens again. Arden storms right back out, dressed now in a pair of jeans and a lumpy sweatshirt.

He looks tense and completely unapproachable, but Nino hurries after him as he stalks into the entry hall and shrugs into his coat.

"Where are you going?" Nino demands, watching Arden collect his keys and yank open the door.

"Anywhere but here."

"Arden, it's the middle of the night. You can't mean to—"

Nino's protests are cut off by the door slamming shut, rattling the frame and making his heart shudder in his chest. Guilt blossoms and spreads, a block of dry ice sending smoky tendrils out through his entire body, turning his limbs sluggish and his thoughts hazy. He can't remember feeling this wretched in his entire life. This time, when his vision smears and sheens, he doesn't fight the tears.

"*Fuck*," he gasps, hollow and shaking.

He startles at a tug on the cuff of his pajama bottoms, and glances down to find Toast squirming around his ankle. When Nino holds his hand down toward her, she leaps up with a flutter of wings and twines herself around his arm.

Nino blinks to clear his vision and finds wide eyes peering up at him, a surprisingly human expression of worry reflecting in all that gold. She's kneading restlessly at his sleeve, and Nino can't even bring himself to mind the sharp little sting as her claws tighten and relax.

"Yeah, I don't know," he says, as though she's asked him a proper question. Pigeon is still looped loosely around his neck, humming quiet little noises of concern. He doesn't know who he's trying to reassure when he says, "Don't worry. Arden will be back. I'm sure he will."

He needs to believe it. This can't be how their friendship ends.

*

Nino falls asleep on the couch, so wrung out that even the inward tumble of his anxieties can't keep him conscious. He wakes a few hours later, with sunlight glaring into his eyes and Ishiko pounding on his front door.

"What are you doing here?" he asks when he lets her in, stepping aside to let her pass.

She glares with startling ire. "Arden is sulking on my couch, and he won't tell me what's wrong."

Nino blinks, taken aback by the aggression in her tone, instinctively trying to squash his guilt so she won't see it in his eyes. "Why are you angry at me?"

"Because I've been trying to call you all morning!" she snaps. "Nino, what the hell?

Why is Arden so upset? Are *you* okay? What is going on?"

"Oh." Nino didn't realize he's been missing calls, only registering now that his phone is still in his room—probably slag, if the fire reached his bedside table. No wonder Ishiko is alarmed. Nino may be a hermit, but he never ignores his friends on purpose.

"*Nino.*" Ishiko grabs his arm and gives it an exasperated shake. Belatedly, Nino lets the front door click shut and leads the way deeper into the apartment. He's still mulling over what to tell her when she asks, "Did you have a fight?"

"You could say that." Nino sits gingerly, trying not to wake Toast and Pigeon where they're curled in a sleepy tangle on the back of the couch. Ishiko follows his lead, claiming the far cushion, keeping her eyes on Nino all the while. The dragons don't stir.

"What happened?" Ishiko asks more quietly, worry softening the anger from her voice.

Nino hesitates, uncertain. He can't tell her about his magic, which means he can't explain why Arden is angry. But considering she came all the way here, presumably leaving Arden alone at her condo in order to confront Nino, she won't be put off without an answer.

Finally, not at all confident in his ability to deflect a deeper interrogation, Nino says, "There was a fire. It started in my room."

Ishiko's eyes widen, white showing around deep umber irises. "Holy shit, Nino."

"It wasn't a *big* fire. No one got hurt." He swallows hard, praying she doesn't ask anything specific about the scope of the conflagration or the damage done. "But it freaked Arden out."

"How on earth did a fire start in your room?"

Nino doesn't answer, but his gaze drifts to the dragons, adorable and snuffling in their sleep.

"Oh," Ishiko breathes. "Well, shit."

"Yeah." Nino rubs the pad of his thumb up Pigeon's snout and over the top of her head, making her crest shiver and flex, but not waking her. "She didn't do it on purpose, and I doubt it will happen again." This may be wishful thinking, but it feels truthful just the same. Pigeon may not be quick and clever in the same ways as her sister, but she was terrified of the unexpected fire. Now she knows it can happen, Nino hopes she'll be more careful. Between his own magic and the fire extinguishers, he's willing to take that gamble.

He also recognizes that this is exactly the leverage he needs to convince Arden the dragons can't stay, but somehow the thought doesn't make him feel any better.

Maybe because he's currently trapped in the limbo of wondering whether he still has a roommate and best friend.

"Is there anything I can do?" Ishiko asks. The caution in her voice tells Nino she knows there's something more going on, but she doesn't push for answers he can't give.

"No." He shakes his head, then reconsiders. "Or... maybe? Do you think you can convince Arden to come home? I need to talk to him."

Her stare turns downright piercing, and Nino fights not to squirm beneath the inescapable weight of her regard. Finally she says, "Sure. I'll tell him to get his ass home."

Nino waits until she's gone and the door is locked behind her before heading into his bedroom to investigate the damage. He's surprised when he flips the switch by the door and the light actually turns on—and even more shocked to realize the damage isn't all that bad. His bed has been reduced to broken beams and dusty cinders, and his bedside table hasn't fared much better, but the fire didn't make it any further. The window is intact, if charred, and the walls and ceiling bear streaks of soot but no structural damage. His magic will easily be able to conceal those marks, if a sponge and soap can't do the trick.

There will be no salvaging his bed frame or mattress, or the bedside table with its ruined contents. Nino's phone is on the floor, burnt and melted to the point it's barely recognizable.

He sighs and takes what's left of his phone in hand. He wishes his magic could fix it, but there's no way. He doesn't have that kind of finesse. It's one thing to put something simple back together, like Arden's favorite coffee mug, which Nino saved that first day and has repaired more than once since the dragons moved in. Like the porcelain figurine of a unicorn his mom kept on the mantle when Nino was little, broken not long after he first started using magic—he was a clumsy child, though he had nothing on Pigeon—and fused back together in a rush of guilty instinct, perfect except for the way he reattached one of the legs backwards.

But he's never been able to do anything with complicated electronics. Even if he straightens the distorted shape of the device back into a proper rectangle—even if he unmelts the protective case and repairs the cracked camera lenses—he has no hope of making the device function.

Just one more piece of his life that Nino has broken beyond repair.

Chapter Seven

The long day crawls by with no sign of Arden, and with each passing hour Nino feels his heart clench tighter.

Pigeon is impossibly clingy once she wakes, smothering in her refusal to abandon Nino for her usual perches. Toast, by contrast, prowls the apartment as though searching for Arden, clearly on edge despite the fact that she was awake when he stormed off. They're both absorbing Nino's anxiety, and he does his best to adopt an air of calm he does not feel, to help them settle down.

He doesn't bother trying to deal with the mess in his bedroom. He'll need help carrying the ruined pieces of furniture down to the building's trash room, and anyway, he's not keen on leaving the dragons unattended while they're so riled up. God only knows what mischief they might cause if they get it into their heads that both of their humans have disappeared.

He does order a replacement for his ruined phone, with a sigh of regret over his checking account balance. Then he goes right back to pacing the living room, replaying every second of last night's disastrous conversation in his head, waiting and waiting and waiting for Arden to come home.

It's nearly sunset when Nino finally hears footsteps in the hallway and the click of the front door. He scrambles up from the couch so quickly both dragons fall out of his lap, fluttering their wings to right themselves as they land lightly on the floor.

Arden rounds the corner looking every bit as grim and sullen as he did when he left. He's still refusing to meet Nino's eyes—a stubbornness that holds even when Nino breathes Arden's name like a plea—his silence as angry as any shouting match. Without so much as an acknowledging glance, Arden storms past Nino and disappears into his room.

The click of the door feels heavy and final, but Nino doesn't allow himself to be cowed. Never mind his own lingering guilt, his fears both rational and otherwise, his emotional and physical exhaustion. He knows in his heart that this confrontation cannot wait, and he hurries after Arden and knocks on the closed door.

He's anticipating a gruff, *Go away*, but he's greeted with silence instead.

He knocks harder. "Arden?"

Still nothing.

When Nino tries the doorknob, he is unsurprised to find the door locked.

"Arden." He tries to inject stubbornness and command into his voice, as he presses a hand to the smooth woodgrain. Rays of sunset pour across his hand from the window on the other side of the living room, painting both his skin and the wood beneath his touch in glaring light. "Please let me in. We need to talk. It's important."

When Arden still doesn't answer, Nino considers his options, all of them imperfect. The respectful thing would be to leave Arden alone. Allow him this perfectly justified sulk and try again in the morning. After all, Nino hasn't been invited in.

But Arden still hasn't responded, not even to demand Nino fuck off. And maybe it's petty to let this fact guide his actions, but Nino doesn't fight the instinct.

"Right. If you're going to be a complete spud about it, I'm letting myself in." He's more than half hoping the jab will goad Arden into saying something—even if it's only an irate, *Did you just call me a potato?*—but when the silence persists, Nino curls his fingers more surely around the doorknob and extends his senses to the mechanism beneath his hand. It's finicky, but nothing beyond his capabilities, and Nino lets out a sigh as he uses magic to unlock the door.

Arden doesn't even seem to notice when he lets himself in, and the stubbornness of this facade grates over Nino's awareness like sandpaper.

Across the room—a master suite nearly twice as large as Nino's bedroom—a queen-sized bed sits tucked directly beneath a large window. Arden lies on his back beside that window, sprawled atop a messy chaos of blankets that he obviously didn't bother putting to rights before running away. His head rests on a blue pillow, and he's laced his fingers together over his stomach. The corners of his mouth curl sullenly downward as he scowls at the ceiling.

Nino tries to close the door quickly enough to prevent Toast and Pigeon from following him, but the dragons slither past his feet. He considers collecting them and forcing them back out into the living room, but there's little point. He would never succeed without using magic—they're too fast—and it feels far too soon to rub Arden's nose in that kind of demonstration, when Nino's magic is the whole reason they're at this impasse in the first place.

Besides, it's not as though the dragons can participate in the conversation. So Nino lets them skitter across the floor, their claws clicking until they reach the small rug that runs alongside Arden's bed.

By the time Nino hoists himself up to sit cross-legged at the foot of the mattress, near Arden's stocking-clad feet, both dragons have burrowed into the disordered bedclothes.

Nino swallows past the lump of emotion threatening to clog his throat, then speaks the most urgent truth that's been gnawing at him all day. "Of course I didn't think you would hate me. I shouldn't have said that."

A beat of silence lingers too long, and Arden continues to glare at the ceiling when he finally answers, "But you were scared to tell me about your magic."

"Yes." It's a painful concession, but Nino already knows he won't get anywhere with lies and half-truths. "I was terrified."

"Of me?" The words are barely more than a whisper. Arden looks strangely regal in the less direct light of the sunset creeping through his window, the curtains pushed aside to reveal the sky and an uneven horizon of buildings leading toward the river. His eyes are wet, and Nino wants desperately to hug him and take everything back, to make all of this okay somehow.

"No," he says, voice thick with emotion. "I wasn't scared of you."

"Then *why*?" Arden demands more fiercely.

Nino has never seen his best friend look so devastated, and it takes every scrap of willpower to keep his own posture loose when his instinct is to huddle in and make himself as small as possible. He resists the urge to fold his knees toward his chest and wrap his arms around them. Considering Arden's questions, such a pose wouldn't be reassuring, and the last thing Nino can afford to do now is shut Arden out.

"Because I didn't want things to change," Nino admits softly, studying the heavy line of Arden's brow, the unhappy set of his full lips, the faint acne scars on his cheek. Nino's voice has gone ragged, and the words tumble out of him, faster and faster in a tangle of confession and plea. "I knew they would. I knew *everything* would change. The longer I kept my secrets, the more impossible it was to say anything. How could you possibly trust me, if you found out I'd been lying for years? For the entire time you've known me? And if you can't trust me, will you even want to be friends? What if you decide to leave? What if you never want to see me again?"

By the time Nino has finished, his heart is pounding so loudly it's a wonder it doesn't drown out every word.

Arden is finally looking at him, but his attention isn't a relief. Not when Arden is staring like Nino has lost his entire mind.

Silence takes them. Endless, agonizing silence. It burrows beneath Nino's skin, tenses his shoulders, makes him huddle in on himself despite his best intentions.

When Arden still doesn't speak, Nino's own voice shatters the silence. "Will you *say something?*"

But Arden, maddening as ever, instead sits up slowly, paying no apparent mind to the way his movements jostle the dragons who are both watching him closely. Nino watches Arden too, wary of the surprisingly graceful maneuver and desperate to know what it means.

When Arden scoots down the mattress and reaches for him, he startles so badly he probably would've fallen off the bed if not for the hug already enveloping him. Nino gasps at being crushed to Arden's chest, his arms trapped between them, hands squashed against Arden's collarbone as his best friend holds onto him so tightly that for a moment he can't breathe.

He squeaks a breathless laugh but doesn't try to pull free. Who needs oxygen anyway?

It's not the easiest angle for a hug, sitting side-by-side—hip to hip—Arden's chin digging sharply into Nino's shoulder and Nino's face squashed into the hollow of Arden's throat. But Nino melts anyway, relaxing his whole body into the embrace. The contact is grounding, and more reassuring than he ever plans to admit. Nino figures out how to drag air into his lungs a moment later, despite the suffocating circle of Arden's arms. Hope wriggles around behind his ribs for the first time all day.

The hug lasts so long that Nino starts to feel over-warm. It's an eternity before he finally gives a reluctant push, easing a little extra space between their bodies.

He opens his eyes—when the hell did he close them?—but can't seem to lift his gaze any higher than the place his fingers splay across the collar of Arden's shirt.

Arden lets go, leaving him unexpectedly bereft. But then strong hands frame Nino's face, tipping his head back and refusing to let him hide. Arden meets his eyes with piercing intensity, staring Nino down like he's searching for answers. The attention is downright intimidating, even knowing Arden as well as he does, and Nino twists his fingers helplessly in the fabric of Arden's shirt.

For a very long time, Arden holds Nino trapped like this, as though even his silence has a point to make. Or perhaps he's planning his words more carefully than he ever has before.

Finally, without letting go, Arden speaks with a calm so measured it must be costing him deliberate effort. "You're not going to lose me." He pauses to draw a shaky breath. "I'm angry at you. I don't think I've *ever been* this angry at you. But I'm not going anywhere."

Quick as that, Nino's eyes start to burn, the hot prickle an inevitable prelude to tears.

"Stubborn," he mutters. But he's smiling, shaken and sheepish, and he can feel the expression scrunching up his whole face. He probably looks ridiculous, but he's so relieved he doesn't care.

Arden rolls his eyes, exaggerating the expression as he drops his hands into his lap. "You're one to talk."

The dragons seem to take the sudden easing of tension as an invitation, darting across the mattress toward Arden, a rush so clumsy they keep knocking each other over. When Arden's gaze darts down to study them with an affectionate little smile, Nino takes the reprieve to scrub his eyes dry. It wouldn't take much to tip him right back over the edge or make him actually cry, but he feels miles better now than he did ten minutes ago. Still worried, unable to shake that familiar fear of everything changing now that Arden knows, but no longer terrified of losing him.

No longer scared that Arden's anger will be the thing that shatters the most important relationship of Nino's life.

That thought gives him pause, sudden and startling as it is. It probably shouldn't. Hell, it's not like he can be surprised Arden means the world to him. But there's a depth to the way the emotion is hitting him now, and it's terrifying in whole different ways from the ones that kept Nino on edge all day.

"Will you show me?" Arden asks, interrupting the disoriented spin of his thoughts.

Nino's brow furrows. "Show you what?"

"Your magic." Arden peers impatiently into his face like Nino is being uncooperative on purpose. "I want to see."

"You've already seen my magic," Nino protests, not bothering to conceal his bewilderment.

"I haven't, really." A grudging smile twitches at one corner of Arden's mouth, so much better than the frown of just a short while before. "Putting out the fire... You didn't have a choice about that. I want to see you do something on purpose. Just for me."

Nino considers—not *whether* to humor Arden's request, but *how*—and then cups his hands together in the space between them, palms up and steady. He can feel Arden watching him with curiosity, fascination, maybe something else he's not quite sure how to read. He does his best to shut Arden's reactions out of his head for the moment, the better to focus on what he is actually doing.

Gathering light into his hands is a lot like gathering warmth around him. He isn't creating anything that isn't already there, just manipulating the elements within reach. There's nothing useful or practical about the magic he is weaving now, but it comes to him easily. After all, this was some of the earliest magic he taught himself, the first he deliberately practiced after learning to consciously control the more instinctive things he can do.

He collects a shimmering amalgam of light between his palms, the electric glow from the overhead bulb offering only a faint pale edge to the more colorful and powerful hues of the sunset emanating through the window. All of it grows brighter once Nino is touching it, holding it, like a cluster of embers whispering into flame where he cradles the gleaming, ephemeral softness. Once he has enough, he shapes it. The stuff is more malleable than clay, barely there at all, and his mind tugs and twists and does not stop until he holds a cascading handful of tiny flowers.

Lilacs. As the wilder green of Nino's magic fades, the ephemeral flowers pulse with the deepening purple of the sunset, their light reflecting in the dizzy blue of Arden's eyes.

There is awe in Arden's stillness. And when he finally lifts one hand to brush his fingers over a cluster of blossoms, his movements are endearingly careful.

He touches the flowers as though he expects them to be real, and Nino laughs delightedly as Arden's fingers pass through the shapes and scatter them. Arden's cheeks are flushed, his lips barely parted, and he stares at Nino's hands as the illusion dissolves into the air.

"How does it work?" Arden breathes, and the awe in his voice makes Nino shiver. "What does it feel like?"

"I have no idea how to answer either of those questions," Nino says, then tries anyway. "It's instinct, mostly. I don't remember the first time I moved something just by thinking about it. Just by wanting to. I was younger than most, but it works the same for everyone as far as I know. You can practice. Improve. Pick up new tricks. Everyone with magical talent has at least one magical parent, but it's not really a system to be learned. There are no schools or teachers or rules. People write things down, but books won't do any good for someone who doesn't have the talent to begin with. And... as for how it feels..."

Nino's not sure why this should be the harder question, but when he tries to find words for how magic makes him feel, he stumbles and stalls out.

Arden looks away. "You don't have to tell me, if it's too private."

"It's not that. It's just really hard to describe. I've never tried putting it into words before. Everyone I've ever talked to about magic already knows."

Arden glowers, perhaps at the implication that there are people Nino has talked to about this who are not him, but he doesn't interrupt.

"It feels good," Nino says finally, not surprised when the words make Arden roll his eyes. He doesn't let the gesture dissuade him from continuing, "Like having more than five senses. Like everything around you is so much more alive than most people realize, and you've got this bright, warm secret inside you because *you* can see the whole of it."

The secret is lonely, too. Especially here in the city, in the life Nino has made far away from his family, this place surrounded by people who don't truly see him. But it's a beautiful secret nonetheless, and before he met Arden, Nino never had a single qualm about keeping it.

This time when Arden turns his gaze away, his expression looks distinctly overwhelmed. His cheeks, pale and prone to sunburns, blaze with a flush so deep that Nino doesn't know what to make of it. He looks flustered, and a little bit lost, and Nino wonders if talking about *secrets* hits too close to home in this moment.

Nino is bracing for Arden's next words to be an attack. They won't be deliberately cruel—that's not Arden's style—but Nino's heart is already fragile and exposed. He's not sure he can abide accusations or anger. He has shown Arden too much. He can't take any of it back now. And no matter how he racks his brain for a way to lighten the mood, Nino comes up short.

"Hang on," Arden blurts, suddenly staring at Nino again. "I asked you to impress me with magic, and you made me a glowing bouquet of flowers. You are such a sap."

"Oh my god, shut up," Nino says, but a relieved grin spreads across his face, and he doubts he could stop smiling if he wanted to. "You loved the flowers. And if you make fun of me, I won't do it again."

Arden snorts, and reaches up to ruffle Nino's hair. Nino makes the obligatory noises of protest, but he enjoys the way Arden's touch lingers just a heartbeat too long—like Nino isn't the only one searching for their lost equilibrium.

Like maybe they'll be okay after all.

Chapter Eight

"Don't be ridiculous, Nino," Arden says, hours later. "You're not sleeping on the couch."

"It's a perfectly nice couch," Nino points out. And it really is—one of the few items of furniture to have survived the dragons with only superficial damage, thanks to how solid and sturdy it is. The upholstery has been scratched all to hell, but the cushions are still soft, and the couch is wide enough for Nino to recline without his feet dangling over the edge.

He's not especially looking forward to sleeping on it, despite this fact. Even the comfiest couch can't compete with an actual bed. But it's also not some great hardship to be endured.

"Why are you being obstinate?" Arden peers at Nino with his jaw set stubbornly, hands on his hips in an imperious pose that makes him look taller than he actually is. The intimidating effect is largely undermined by the fact that he's wearing a pair of soft flannel pajama bottoms and a t-shirt featuring some cartoon villain Nino doesn't recognize. "It's not like we haven't shared before. Let's just get some sleep, and I'll buy you a new bed tomorrow."

Nino's eyes narrow. It's silly to be affronted—he and Arden have been mingling their finances for years, and he knows just how much money his friend has available to throw around—but he still fails to bite back his protest. "I don't need you to buy me a bed."

"Of course you don't *need me to.*" Arden throws his hands skyward in an exasperated gesture that jostles Toast on his shoulder.

Nino can tell how hard he's trying not to be snappish, and suspects Arden is having a difficult time keeping a complicated jumble of anger at bay. "But it's only fair, considering my dragons destroyed half your bedroom."

"*Your* dragons?" Nino squawks. He snaps his mouth shut too late, teeth clenching as though if he grinds them hard enough he can call the words back.

Arden blinks, startled. Then a slow, smug smile spreads across his face. God, he looks so pleased, so tauntingly satisfied as he crosses his arms over his broad chest.

"I just assumed," Arden drawls, cocky smirk transforming his handsome features into something that would probably get him punched in a bar, "since you keep claiming you want nothing to do with them. But we can share custody if you like. If you ask nicely."

"We've been friends for ten years," Nino grouses. "How do you keep finding new ways to be insufferable?"

"It's a gift," Arden retorts cheerfully.

Well. Now Nino is definitely sleeping on the couch. He's not giving Arden the satisfaction of any more victories tonight.

"I almost died. You have to be nice to me." He intends the words to be funny—he didn't come anywhere near almost dying—but perhaps he should've realized just how scared Arden was, waking up to a fire in their home and Nino right at ground zero. As soon as the words are out of Nino's mouth, Arden's smile evaporates, his expression turning dangerous and still.

"I'm sorry." Nino takes a stumbling step forward, hovering just beyond Arden's personal space, not sure why he's hesitating to close the last of the distance and hug his friend. "Arden, I'm sorry, I shouldn't have said that. It wasn't even that close."

"It was, though." Arden's voice comes low and gruff, thick with emotion.

Before Nino can think of any way to answer his best friend's grim intensity, Arden's hand darts out and grabs Nino's forearm, lifting and turning it with gentle purpose, revealing the deep bruise from Nino's fall. Arden stares down at the mottled mess of sickly yellow and burnished purple, his expression one of ferocious displeasure.

The fingers of Arden's free hand ghost across the spot, and Nino squashes the desire to snatch his arm back. Somehow, he doubts Arden will see reason if he tries to point out that it's just a bruise—it's not a big deal—he doesn't need his best friend hovering like some overprotective mother hen.

"It was exactly that close," Arden insists without releasing him. "What if you hadn't woken up in time? What if you hadn't been able to put out the fire?"

"Then *you* would have put it out," Nino explains reasonably. Wasn't that the point of the extra fire extinguishers? "And Pigeon woke me in plenty of time."

He startles when Arden drags him into a rough, tight hug, but he doesn't hesitate to hold on right back.

"Please stop being stubborn." Arden's words come out muffled in the fabric of Nino's shirt. "My bed's big enough to share. This doesn't have to be weird just because I'm angry at you."

Nino's not sure how to explain that Arden's anger isn't the reason this feels weird, so he doesn't try. "Okay. But the dragons have to sleep in the living room." He doubts Pigeon will repeat last night's accident, and Toast seems to have given up for the time being on her efforts to ignite the furniture, but Nino will feel better knowing that any potential fires are far enough away to give him a head start.

"Deal," Arden agrees, and drags Nino to bed.

*

It takes a remarkable amount of effort to keep the dragons out long enough to close the bedroom door. In the end Nino has to resort to magic, which feels like cheating—especially when Toast and Pigeon voice a perfectly matched pair of baleful yowls, as he finally traps them on the other side of the door and sets the lock.

"Well, now I feel like a monster," Nino mutters, flopping down on the closer half of the mattress and flinging an arm over his eyes.

"Never." Arden crawls over him to reach the other side, rather than simply walking around and climbing over the foot of the bed. He nudges Nino's shin with his bare toes, then wriggles under the covers. "You might be a very talented freak, but never a monster."

Nino huffs, and then follows Arden's lead, burying himself beneath the bedclothes and stretching out on his back with a sigh of relief.

"Um?" he mumbles when Arden's arm drapes across his stomach, bringing a press of unexpected heat along his side. He lowers his arm and opens his eyes, and finds Arden watching him with a confusing tangle of curiosity and worry. Arden's proximity leaves Nino dizzy for a moment, and it takes him several seconds to manage, "And you called *me* a sap."

"Shut up," Arden mutters, and there's something so growly and sweet in the words that Nino sets his hand over Arden's wrist and leaves it there. He more than half expects Arden to wriggle away now that he's made his point, but he stays, a little too close, studying Nino's face like he's searching for something.

"Are you alright?" Nino asks finally, when the silence has stretched long enough to turn uncomfortable.

"Yes," Arden says. Then, "No. Maybe."

"Glad we cleared that up," Nino teases.

Arden's expression doesn't lighten. If anything, he looks even more pensive than before. Finally he asks, "Why did you never tell me?"

Nino resists the urge to point out that they've already had this conversation. That he already hurt Arden's feelings by admitting how terrified he was at the prospect. There's a deeper weight to the question, beyond Nino and Arden and the decade of lies between them. This isn't Arden's anger asking. It's a genuine effort to understand, when Nino has given him almost nothing to work with.

"It wasn't about you," Nino says softly.

Arden arches one eyebrow at this apparent contradiction, an expression so dry and skeptical that Nino huffs a nearly soundless laugh.

"It wasn't *entirely* about you," he amends. "Or about me, for that matter. This secret doesn't just belong to me. It's not my place to confide it." Nino is aware this makes him a hypocrite. He made his choices anyway. And now that he understands it won't cost him his best friend, he can't bring himself to regret being known.

"Why?" Arden presses, genuinely perplexed. "Why is it something you need to hide in the first place?"

Nino shrugs helplessly. "Magic is only safe if it's secret."

"Even from me?" Arden asks quietly, and Nino's heart gives a protective pulse. Of course Arden still doesn't understand. The man may be stubborn and entitled and remarkably arrogant, but he is also impossibly sweet. Good and sincere right down to his core. Arden is the sort of man who could never intend harm to anyone— who rushes to make amends when he learns he's fucked up—who stumbles often, but always course corrects along the way, and tries with every breath to do right by other people.

Of course a man like that is struggling with the notion that protecting a world of magic meant guarding the information even from him.

"You should've trusted me with this," Arden laments.

"It was never a question of trust, you stubborn lump." Nino gives Arden's wrist a squeeze to soften the rebuke. He even refrains from rolling his eyes. "Not the way you're thinking. It's about the habits that protect us. When you grow up being told nobody can ever know how special you are—that it's not safe—that everyone is depending on you to keep your mouth shut no matter what... It's not easy to cross that line."

"Is the world so dangerous for people with magic?"

"Yes," Nino answers without hesitation. "And not just for the people. For all of the other magical creatures too. The dragons, and the merfolk, and the unicorns. Anyone who fails to guard the secret is putting every single one of us at risk."

"But magic is amazing!" Arden protests, breathless and insistent.

"Yes," Nino grins. "Obviously. But think of it like... Suppose I wasn't a warlock. Let's pretend I'm a visitor from another planet, and I can do lots of things humans can't. What happens the second the population knows I exist?"

Arden seems to genuinely and very intently consider before answering, "I suppose the government takes an interest and it's not long before you disappear." Then, after an even longer stretch of pensive quiet—one Nino knows better than to interrupt—Arden asks, "Do you really think that's what would happen with magic?"

"I don't know." Nino chews on his lower lip as he considers. "I hope not. But the government isn't the only possible source of harm. And I don't get to take that gamble for every magical person and creature on the planet. Telling is taboo for a reason."

"Huh."

"You still look confused," Nino observes, though the wounded edge is finally gone from Arden's expression, leaving a less intense air of curiosity in its wake.

"Who enforces these rules?" Arden asks. It's not any of the questions Nino expected.

"They're not rules, exactly." He studies the deep, piercing blue of Arden's eyes and tries to figure out how to explain. His efforts aren't helped by how tired he is—after a nearly sleepless night and an emotional roller coaster of a day—but he soldiers on. "It's more like a shared understanding."

"Sounds dubious," Arden mutters, and Nino chuckles.

"Maybe. There's no governing body in charge, or anything like that. No laws or treaties or enforcement agencies. It's more like pockets of magic. Places that are safe. And anyone living outside those places does their best to avoid drawing attention."

Arden leans closer, arm tightening around Nino in what feels like an involuntary movement. His crowding warmth is making Nino feel safe and sleepy, which in turn makes it more difficult to focus on the words coming out of Arden's mouth.

"How many are there? People with magic?"

"No idea." Nino shrugs one shoulder and offers a wry smile. "We exist all over the world. It's not like there's a magical rolodex with everyone's contact information."

"What? Magic users don't use social media?" Arden teases—then looks startled and blurts, "Wait. *You* don't have social media. Is that a magic thing? I thought you were just a hopeless recluse."

"I'm not a recluse. But yeah, social media is the opposite of avoiding attention. I don't know about anyone else, but I'd rather not tempt fate."

"Probably wise," Arden mutters. "I can only imagine what sorts of trouble you'd get into."

"You're one to talk!" But before Nino can bolster his point by reminding Arden how difficult it was to keep him from posting dragon photos all over the internet, he cuts himself off with a long, huge yawn that he can't hide even when he covers his mouth with the back of his hand. When he puts his arm down, his eyes are drooping, fatigue finally overtaking him.

Arden's attention is still on Nino, an unfamiliar smile twitching at one corner of his generous mouth. Nino wants to ask why he's smiling, but a heavy blanket of sleep is closing in around him, and he can't even manage a *thank you* when Arden leans over him to turn off the bedside lamp.

Chapter Nine

It's the middle of the night when Nino tumbles out of an incomprehensible dream into sudden, disorienting wakefulness. Confusion rushes through him as he takes in the unfamiliar shadows of the room around him. He's lying on his side near the edge of the mattress, multiple pillows squashed under his head as usual, but those aren't his bookshelves—not packed as they are with all the thick, bright spines of an expansive collection of fantasy novels. That's not where the door should be, either. There's an alarm clock on the bedside table, the numbers glowing red. Even the desk is wrong, sturdy and dark and too far away.

And the warmth along his back is far too solid to be his own body heat collected by heavy blankets.

When Nino shifts in place, he registers the arm around his waist a second before it tightens. He shivers at a soft tickle of breath across his nape, and his mind whirls with a refrain of, *What the hell?*

He hasn't gone out in weeks. Surely he would remember going home with someone last night.

There's no falling back asleep now. Nino huffs a long, low breath and braces himself to turn around—but halfway through adjusting his position, his brain catches up with the fact that this doesn't smell like a stranger's room. He knows the soft, clean scent of the same detergent he uses himself, plus the faint lavender of his best friend's favorite shampoo, and the subtler undertone that is simply *Arden.*

By the time he finishes wriggling over onto his other side—wishing he weren't quite so close to the edge of the bed—he's no longer confused to find Arden blinking at him with sleep-hazed eyes.

Nino would scoot back and put some distance between them if he could. There is something alarmingly intimate in the way Arden is holding him.

Moonlight pours through the window, where Arden hasn't bothered to pull the curtains shut. It's just enough light to take in Arden's face, blue eyes gone black as midnight as they slit open in the darkness.

"What are you doing in my bed?" Arden asks, except his words are so slurred with sleep that most of the syllables run together into mush, and it's only years of dealing with him during groggy mornings that allows Nino to make sense of the question.

If Nino's heart weren't racing so inexplicably fast in his chest, he might crack a joke about unrestrained debauchery. Instead, he injects dry disbelief into his voice as he answers, "You insisted. I don't have a bed anymore, remember?"

"Oh." Arden's next blink looks a little more wakeful and a lot more lucid. "Right."

Now that he's on his side facing Arden directly, Nino has very few options for where to put his hands. He refuses to overthink it as he rests them against Arden's broad chest, trying not to get distracted by the quickening rhythm of the heartbeat directly beneath his palm. The warmth between them borders on uncomfortable, heat collected beneath heavy blankets, shared between two bodies that have been snugged together in sleep for several hours. But Nino doesn't mind. And though it must be even worse in those flannel pajamas, Arden doesn't protest either.

Nino wishes he had more than the wash of moonlight to see by, as he studies Arden's face in the surreal balance of soft blue light and deep shadows. His own heart is racing, and he's fast losing his ability to pretend he doesn't know why.

When Nino worries his lower lip between his teeth, Arden's focus slips instantly down to stare at his mouth, lingering for several seconds before jolting back up to Nino's eyes.

Oh, Nino thinks, barely restraining a frantic bubble of laughter. Maybe he doesn't need to pretend.

Maybe he's not the only one feeling something fundamental shift between them.

"Are you going to let go?" he asks, allowing his own gaze to dart down and watch the barely parted seam of Arden's lips, the bob of his throat as Arden swallows.

"Do you want me to let go?" Arden's voice sounds thick with gravel, and Nino's expression twitches into a smile.

"Not especially."

"Good," Arden rasps, his arm already tightening around Nino's waist and reeling him in. Squashed in the space between them, Arden's free hand curls beneath Nino's chin, a bossy and wordless command guiding him in for a first disorienting kiss. It's clumsy, but Nino doesn't care. His fingers twist in the front of Arden's shirt, attempting the impossible task of pulling Arden even closer.

He startles when his friend's weight shifts, and has only a split second to react when Arden starts to *push*—a movement that unambiguously telegraphs his intention to pin Nino beneath him. Nino pushes back instead of letting it happen, breaking from the kiss with a shaky gasp.

Arden retreats immediately. "What's wrong?" His voice carries all the anxious tension of a man who is terrified he fucked up, and Nino couldn't hold back an answering burst of laughter if he tried.

"Nothing is wrong, you sweet, ridiculous oaf." He quiets his mirth with difficulty. "I just don't want you to roll us off the bed. There isn't any mattress behind me."

"Oh." Arden's sheepish expression is adorable.

"Really living up to those disaster-bi credentials, aren't you?" Nino teases, affection shining so fiercely inside him that it's a wonder the room doesn't light up.

"Stop talking." As retorts go, the words alone aren't terribly effective. But then Arden takes firm hold of Nino and rolls the other way, onto his back, dragging Nino gamely along with him. Nino lets himself be manhandled, delighted and dizzy. And when he finds himself kneeling astride Arden's hips, he decides this is a very nice place to be. Not quite as thrilling as the notion of Arden's muscular bulk squashing him into the mattress, but perfect in its own distinct way. He has a much better view of Arden's face now, more moonlight than shadow, and the glint of emotion in Arden's eyes is enough to take Nino's breath away.

He wonders how he looks to Arden in this moment. The blankets fall away behind him and let in chilly air, pleasant after the shared cocoon of excess heat. The thin fabric of his t-shirt offers no insulation at all, and he shivers, maybe from the cold, maybe from the intimate slide of Arden's gaze along his lanky frame.

Then Arden is reaching for him, one hand curling hard at his hip, the other tangling in his hair. Nino tumbles eagerly forward, covering Arden's body, his mouth, taking a second greedy kiss without hesitation.

By the time he registers a stiffening nudge between his legs, Nino's own body burns with answering urgency. There's nothing suave in the way he shifts in search of friction, giddy at how good it feels despite somehow being not enough. He doesn't have the leverage he needs, even as he rubs harder—even when both of Arden's hands grip Nino's hips with steely strength and drag him down—even as every movement turns frantic between them, and the kiss breaks in favor of a panting need for air.

It's still not enough. And when Arden steadies Nino and rolls them over again— putting Nino on his back in the middle of the mattress, safely away from the edge of the bed—his relief is so powerful he could cry.

Considering what an inferno Arden was beneath him a moment ago, Nino isn't surprised to see him sit back on his heels and drag the shirt off over his head. The maneuver is smooth and efficient, and Nino stares at the broad expanse of Arden's bare chest, at the sturdy muscles and dusting of hair.

It's unreasonable for anyone to be so effortlessly sexy, especially *Arden*, who is supposed to be Nino's aggravating dork of a best friend, not the stuff of his dirtiest fantasies.

But apparently Arden is going to be both from now on, because Nino can't make himself look away.

Before Nino can embarrass himself by saying something alarmingly sappy, Arden is on him again, crushing him into the mattress and kissing him senseless. Nino still doesn't have any leverage, but he doesn't need it anymore. Not at this infinitely better angle, with Arden bearing down on top of him, heavy and firm and impossibly intimate between Nino's legs. When Arden's hips rut forward, the shock of pleasure draws a cry from Nino's chest, the sound muffled around the possessive thrust of Arden's tongue. *This* is exactly the friction he needs, the craving he couldn't sate in his previous position.

Part of him wants to be more naked. To take this slower, to touch and explore, to taste Arden everywhere. But more urgent instincts are too impatient for anything beyond this, Arden moving against him, passion and heat and overwhelming strength, as Nino arches and squirms to meet him.

When even this isn't quite enough, Nino wraps his legs around Arden's waist. Arden breaks from the kiss with a huff of laughter, and then his mouth is moving along Nino's throat instead. Mapping and marking him. Making Nino whimper.

He digs his heels into the small of Arden's back to goad him faster. Nino's touch roams, worshipful and restless, as their rhythm turns more frantic. He slides his hands along Arden's jaw, his nape, the strong slope of his back. Tangling his fingers in Arden's distractingly soft hair, he pulls Arden away from tasting the hollow of Nino's throat, up into another kiss.

They finish like that, clinging to each other without apology. Arden's growl of satisfaction cuts through the quiet darkness, and Nino's cry muffles in the crook of his shoulder a moment later.

Nino can't remember the last time he came in his pants, but even as he drifts hazily down from the heat of the moment, he can't bring himself to regret the mess they just made. Not when he feels boneless and sated, his body pleasantly tired, his senses alight with every detail of Arden surrounding him.

Arden's breath, hot and uneven against the side of Nino's neck, gradually begins to slow. His weight feels different now that there is stillness between them—a softer sort of closeness—a surreal and welcome quiet, only a little bit awkward.

Nino doesn't want to let go. He unwinds his legs only reluctantly from around Arden's waist, then hums a pleased little sound when Arden presses a lingering kiss below his jaw.

It takes Nino a very long time to suggest, "We should probably get cleaned up." He doesn't really want to. He's enjoying the way Arden feels like some sort of impossibly heavy heated blanket on top of him.

"In a minute," Arden mumbles, burrowing in tighter.

Nino smiles at the ceiling. His fingers move idly through Arden's hair, fingertips tracing lazy patterns along Arden's scalp. He thinks he could stay here, just like this until the sun rises, and be perfectly content.

A crash from the living room startles them so badly that they bump their heads painfully together, both of them turning to stare at the closed bedroom door.

"Fuck," Arden huffs, pushing up onto his elbows.

"That sounded like the TV again."

A moment later, a pair of fluttery, almost apologetic chirps follow the noise of destruction. Arden reacts to the reassurance that Pigeon and Toast are unhurt by collapsing forward on top of Nino once more. He buries his face in the line of Nino's neck and heaves a long, defeated sigh.

"We really can't keep them, can we." The words aren't pitched as a question, and the resignation makes Nino's heart twinge.

"It's okay." Nino nuzzles Arden's temple, pressing a kiss to his hairline. "I found somewhere to take them. We can start planning our trip tomorrow. I promise they'll be safe."

Chapter Ten

They make the drive all in one long, exhausting push, because they can't very well check into a hotel—even a pet friendly one—and trust a pair of noisy, energetic, rampantly destructive dragons not to draw attention.

The backseat of Arden's car is barely large enough to accommodate the massive pet carrier they're using to keep Toast and Pigeon contained. Nino feels a little guilty for keeping them caged up like this for such a long drive, especially as they've grown increasingly restless, but it's the only safe option. As he sits in the passenger seat wishing he could do at least some portion of the driving, rather than leaving the whole burden to Arden, each skitter and clatter from the pet crate makes him glad the dragons don't have free run of the car. He can too vividly imagine needing his magic to save them all from fiery, high-velocity death if Pigeon managed to wriggle beneath the brake pedal, and he's not sure his reflexes are up to the challenge.

"You okay?" Nino asks, when Arden's been quiet for five miles straight.

"Just thinking," Arden murmurs. It's not an especially troubled tone of voice, so whatever he's pondering can't be anything too heavy. Hell, he hasn't been shy about asking questions during the past few days, as he and Nino wrangled the logistics of a spontaneous and extremely clandestine road trip to the middle of Canada. Questions about magic. About Nino. About Nino's magic.

They've both avoided asking any questions about what the hell this startling new dynamic between them means. It's been easier just to keep sleeping in Arden's bed. Nino's not actually worried. Despite how completely off-guard this caught him, he feels steady and sure in Arden's affections. There is something shockingly natural in the shift from friendship to something else entirely, and he refuses to overthink a good thing.

Well. He refuses to overthink it *much*. Twelve hours is a long time to be trapped in a car, even with his best friend. Even through long stretches of genuinely gorgeous terrain, as the flat and boring parts of central Minnesota gradually gave way to rocky hills and rolling highways that dipped and rose and stretched through colorful forests. Green conifers and the impossible gold-orange-maroon of other trees changing color with the season.

They've driven through the night and straight into morning, Nino keeping Arden awake with a steady supply of coffee and an equally steady deluge of cheerful chatter. Also snacks. Lots of snacks. The soft-sided cooler at Nino's feet is nearly empty now, depleted of its tightly packed stash of sandwiches, cheese sticks, hard boiled eggs, and soda. The coffee is almost gone too, as is the ridiculous quantity of beef jerky Arden packed to keep the dragons sated and distracted.

There will be plenty of time to restock their exhausted reserves. They won't be driving home until tomorrow—a more leisurely pace following a stay in a local hotel—after they see Toast and Pigeon safely settled.

"Do you need more coffee?" Nino asks.

"No thanks." Arden reaches over to set his hand on Nino's leg and gives a soft squeeze. "We're finally in the home stretch. Besides, I suspect pulling over and peeing in these woods might be disrespectful somehow."

"Good instinct," Nino agrees, covering Arden's hand and threading their fingers together in a gesture that still feels daring, despite all the times he's done it.

Nino studies Arden's profile for a moment, taking in how soft he looks in the rising glow of sunrise. Stubble dusts the usually clean-shaven line of his jaw, and his gaze holds attentive on the road despite the obvious fatigue lining his features. Even Arden's hair looks tired somehow, messy and smushed on one side from the restless way he keeps running his fingers through the strands as though to jostle himself awake.

When Arden gives him a wry look, Nino snorts and turns to watch the scenery instead. They're two hours beyond the last proper town of their journey, following a dubious dirt road that looks like it should be bumpy and uninviting, but somehow allows Arden's car to roll smoothly across the terrain unhindered. Even without the breadcrumbs of magic Nino is following with his own extra senses, he would know they're headed the right direction from how easily Arden is maneuvering over deep potholes and shaky gravel.

There is pervasive magic smoothing this road, and protection woven through the tree branches closing in on all sides like a strangely sunny cave.

"Tell me something," Arden says, and when Nino glances over he finds the pensive expression back on Arden's face. "If magic is so powerful and secret, why hasn't anyone used it to take over the world?"

"It wouldn't work," Nino says simply.

"Why not?" Arden presses, clearly not satisfied by the careless reply.

Nino catches his lower lip between his teeth as he considers how best to answer. It's something he's considered before, certainly. After all, people with magic are still *people*, and power is a complicated thing. But he's also never tried putting any of it into words before. He hasn't needed to, when everyone else in his life who possesses magic shares the same fundamental understanding.

His voice is thoughtful when he finally says, "Because doing deliberate harm with magic tends to backfire." He's still covering

Arden's hand with his own, and he adjusts his grip now, slipping beneath Arden's palm so they can hold hands properly. "I'm sure there are people who've tried. It's not like having magic makes you inherently *good*. But even if someone figured out how to wield their talents that way, the cost would be..."

Nino tries to figure out how to put something so innate into words—the inexorable sense of balance he can feel in the place beneath his skin where magic lives—his certainty that if he ever tried to use his talents in pursuit of power, something equally fundamental inside him would swell up like an ocean tide and crush him beneath the waves.

"That bad?" Arden murmurs. He sounds as though he understands, even though Nino hasn't articulated these thoughts aloud. He studies Nino's face with a quick glance before returning his attention to the road. Something in the line of his mouth says he grasps the weight of the thing, even if he cannot possibly understand the scope of what Nino has failed to explain.

Nino shakes off his frustration at the inadequacy of words, and slouches in his seat with a lopsided smile. "You'll just have to trust me that it won't happen, I suppose."

"Of course I trust you." Arden says this so easily. A fact so basic that even Nino's years of half-truths and outright lies can't shake it. And the earnest intensity of the words would have knocked Nino right over if he weren't already sitting down.

Nino wants to answer, but his voice is caught in his chest, tight with feeling, and he closes his eyes. It takes him several seconds to remember how to breathe.

"Is... this the place?" Arden asks, sounding dubious, as the car crunches to a stop on a patch of gravel.

Nino opens his eyes, curious why Arden sounds so underwhelmed and doubtful. What he sees takes his breath away, leaving him more confused than ever at Arden's reaction. Beyond a rickety wooden gate, there are multiple buildings scattered through a truly massive clearing. Nino was expecting something small. Cozy. But this is an entire village, with modern houses, sheds, outbuildings clustered around an ancient-looking castle that reaches so high above the trees that only magic could conceal it from the world.

Oh. *Oh.* He realizes belatedly that the tingle he feels bubbling across his skin is indeed a concealment charm. Ineffectual for him, with his inner wellspring of magic, but Arden has no such defenses.

"Here." Nino squeezes Arden's hand as he sends a wordless pulse of protective magic between them. He watches Arden's face while he does so, enjoying the way Arden's eyes go wide with shock as the true shape of the clearing comes into view.

"Holy shit," Arden gasps.

"Yep." Nino drags his attention away, following Arden's gaze out the windshield. The buildings are still there, and beyond them sprawl vast open spaces. Even at this distance, idling at the farthest edge of the clearing, Nino can see an impossible myriad of life filling the world before him. Not just people and dragons, but other sorts of creatures. A handful of unicorns grazing near a low stone wall. A gryphon, bigger and lovelier than Nino expected from the imperfect illustrations he's seen. Smaller figures, glowing and darting and in some cases hovering right in the air, too minute for his eyes to decipher what they might be.

And of course, dragons. No wonder this sanctuary requires a hiding place of such massive scope. From here, Nino can't make out any dragons near Toast and Pigeon's size—though he's confident the sanctuary takes in creatures of any age who need care and guidance. The dragons he can see range in scale from small bicycle to very large semi-truck. The larger ones must be adults, here to help with the work and necessary care, and the thought makes him smile.

Nino glances toward Arden and finds blue eyes shining with moisture, an expression of untempered awe written across his face.

"*Oh*," Arden breathes. "They really will be safe here."

"Didn't I promise?" Nino teases gently.

Arden grins at him. "Yes. You absolutely did."

Epilogue

Summer will always be Nino's favorite time of year, no matter how much everyone around him grumbles about the stifling weather. Today in particular is downright pleasant, hot but not oppressive, with a sporadic wind that softens the world around him as he makes his way home through a bustling early evening.

He's taken public transit home even though Arden usually gives him a ride these days. He didn't know how late he would be out with his coworkers, meeting up at a bar near the office to celebrate someone's recent promotion. They parted ways earlier than he expected, but Nino's got such an abundance of cheerful energy to burn, he figured he would take the long way home rather than call his boyfriend with the change of plans.

The sun is just beginning to set as Nino steps onto his street, the sky above tall buildings burnishing warm with the first streaks of orange and pink. The sun on the horizon makes him squint, and he rolls his sleeves up a little higher as he walks. His satchel bumps his hip with every step, the weight of his laptop and papers altering his stride just slightly. He catches a glimpse of himself in a bakery window, all lanky limbs and dark hair gone messy after a long day.

He hopes Arden is home, but he hasn't bothered checking in. There's nothing urgent in the feeling—just the constant, familiar hum in his chest of wanting to be around Arden—and Nino will find out soon enough.

His phone vibrates with an incoming call, as he steps into the startling cool of his building's lobby. A quick glance at the name on the screen, and then he lets the call go to

voicemail. He'll call his mom back later.
Maybe tomorrow. He needs to fortify
himself to fend off her increasingly
frequent nudges, about how six years is long
enough to make Arden wait and isn't it time
he married the poor man?

Nino has no idea how to convince her
there's no rush. He and Arden have talked
about it half a dozen times, and sure, they
probably will someday. But not yet. Not now.
Nino has spent the past six years—longer
than that, really, if he's honest—weaving his
magic around Arden. Adoration, a hundred
shared secrets, a devotion that will never
break. Protections that run soul-deep and
permanent. For the moment, nothing else
feels quite as important by comparison.

So Nino ignores his phone, and the buzz
of a voicemail notification a moment later,
and rides the elevator up to his floor in
silence.

The second he pushes his front door
open, he freezes with a hand on the knob.

His grip tightens convulsively, but it's not fear that clatters through him at the powerful pulse of magic across his senses. How can he be scared, when the last time he stumbled into a sensation like this was six years ago, bringing results that were strange and disastrous and ultimately wonderful? This magic—warm and tingling and a little bit skittish—feels impossibly familiar.

"Arden?" he calls, tossing his keys into the small basket beside the door and kicking off his shoes, letting the door swing shut behind him. The weight of humidity in the air suggests the balcony is open and has been for some time, and when Nino listens carefully, he hears a quiet thump he can't place.

"In the office!" Arden calls. His voice carries across the apartment, coming from the room that used to belong to Nino and has since been transformed into a home office.

Nino shrugs off his bag and drops it a little too hard on his way through the living room. His footsteps are quiet as he rushes across his home, feeling ridiculous and incredulous and full of wild hope. He tries to manage his expectations in this tiny fragment of time. Surely there is some other explanation for the magic floating across his awareness, making him feel lighter than air.

Then he reaches the open door, makes it two steps into the office, and yelps in surprise as a sleek, silvery shape barrels into his chest and knocks him down. Nino stumbles, tips over, doesn't quite catch himself. But he miraculously manages to land on his back without hitting his head on the way down. His breath huffs out in a rush when something warm and unyielding, and startlingly heavy, lands on his chest with a kneading pinprick of claws.

He blinks up into enormous gold eyes. The slitted pupils seem to study him with an almost human delight, and Nino's face splits into a grin.

"Pigeon?" God, it has to be. The little chirp in her throat rumbles deeper and louder than he remembers, but it's still somehow the same—and so is the happy little wriggle she makes at the sound of her name, thwapping his hip with her tail, knocking the rest of the air out of Nino's chest as he realizes she's about three times bigger than last time he saw her.

He braces his hands against the floor and levers himself upright with difficulty. A smaller Pigeon would have tumbled down into his lap with a clumsy flutter of wings. This larger, less helpless Pigeon simply moves with him, coiling stubbornly against his chest, craning her neck to keep peering directly into his eyes. After several staring heartbeats, she tilts just slightly to one side and extends the delicate frill around her head.

She quips another rumbly chirrup, then slithers to the floor, an iridescent flash and an elegant roll of her snake-like body, her claws clicking on the hardwood.

Her frill folds back down again, and Nino laughs, scratches beneath her chin until one of her hind legs begins to twitch ecstatically in the air.

Distracted as he is by *one* unexpected dragon, it takes Nino almost a full minute to raise his eyes and take in the rest of the room. He finds Arden perched on the big, adjustable desk chair, sitting in it all wrong—or possibly exactly right—sprawled sideways with one leg tucked to his chest and the other extended over the armrest. Unreasonably pretty, just like always. Then another flash of silver catches Nino's attention, and he lets his gaze follow the glint of reflected sunlight to find Toast sitting perfectly still on the simple day bed that takes up the opposite wall.

The stillness is clearly a momentary interruption, as Toast trills excitedly and then wriggles and rolls with familiar exuberance.

It takes Nino a moment to realize Toast isn't tumbling around alone. The kitten is tumbling with her, scrambling all over Toast like this dragon is exciting new terrain— batting at her frill and chasing the twitch of her tail—darting around between her ankles and being an adorable nuisance.

The other two cats—crotchety old felines with no patience for such energetic antics—sit near the top of the enormous cat tower Arden originally bought for two dragons who cannot possibly fit in those little cubbies anymore. Both cats lounge in their habitual perches, watchful and pretending not to be interested in the drama playing out below.

Nino chuckles but doesn't bother trying to coax them down.

All three cats are rescues. The old ladies came as a pair from a shelter. The kitten is a sweet yet murderous little hellion, simultaneously the best and worst cat Nino has ever known. Arden found her in a dumpster six months ago, and refused to consider parting with her—not that Nino tried very hard to persuade him, once they were sure she didn't already belong to someone else.

Considering Toast has grown even more than Pigeon in the last six years, it's amazing how gentle she's being with the kitten. Her rambunctious playfulness seems contained, in a way that has to be deliberate. Which makes sense, Nino supposes. Six years isn't enough time for a pair of infant dragons to grow up into full-fledged adults, but they clearly aren't babies anymore. And when he glances down at Pigeon again, where she's cuddled up against his side and rumbling a sound very much like a purr, he finds an awareness in her eyes that wasn't there before.

"How on *earth*?" he asks, not sure if he's asking the dragons—who won't be able to answer no matter how intelligent they've grown—or Arden.

"They were in the living room when I got home from work," Arden says, rising from his chair and flopping down beside Nino on the floor. "The balcony door was wide open. They must've let themselves in somehow."

"Magic," Nino explains very helpfully. He thinks of all the times he's used his own talents to unlock doors, for the sake of convenience or nosiness or occasional emergency.

Arden snorts, a sound comprised of equal parts indignation and amusement. His eyes are unrepentantly adoring. A heartbeat of anticipation lingers and softens, and then he leans in, curling his fingers beneath Nino's jaw and tugging him in for a slow kiss.

As greetings go, it's Nino's favorite kind. And despite the distraction of visiting dragons, he lets himself melt into Arden, twisting his fingers in the front of Arden's shirt just to make extra sure he doesn't stop too soon.

"Welcome home," Arden says when the kiss finally ends.

Nino grins at him, bumping their noses together, shaken by all the emotions bouncing around in his chest. He wasn't sure if they would ever see the dragons again—

wasn't sure Toast and Pigeon would even remember them—and this unexpected reunion has his delighted heart ready to burst. That they seem healthy and happy makes him want to cry, elated and completely overwhelmed.

He still makes a mental note to get in touch with the rescue sanctuary just in case, to make sure this isn't a jailbreak situation. But even as he makes these plans, his heart is so full he almost can't stand it.

"Come on." Arden interrupts this whirlwind, tugging Nino upright as he stands from the floor. "It's way past supper time. Let's figure out what teenage dragons eat."

The End

About the Author

Yolande Kleinn may be a shameless dreamer and a stubborn optimist, but she is also a proud purveyor of romance and erotica. Excitable, fastidious and a little eclectic, she spends every spare moment writing the stories she wants to read. If she can drag other people into the pool along with her, then so much the better.

You can find Yolande via her website:
yolandekleinn.com

Other Titles by Yolande

AN INTIMATE CHARADE

Cargo ship captain Galin Odona is in desperate need of a contract. When a lucrative opportunity comes his way, he invites Addison Valdez—smart, stubborn, and the only Human member of his crew— to join the negotiation.

Anatoria Baell's contract is not precisely legal, and she has unconventional methods for choosing where to put her trust. Galin agrees to pose as a distant relation during a gathering at her private estate. The negotiation takes a complicated turn when

Addison proclaims that Galin is not only his captain, but his mate. The hot-headed lie puts them in a tough spot, maintaining their charade for the duration.

But Galin is a terrible liar. Even worse, he's been in love with Addison for years. Now, through tight quarters and an illusion of intimacy, he must win the contract without giving himself away. The task seems monumental, but Galin cannot afford to fail.

ALL THE WAY HOME I'LL BE WARM

Driving home for the holidays, Jamie Phipps can't believe his car has broken down only four hours from the finish line. At least he finds distraction in the arms of a gorgeous older man. When they part ways, Jamie hopes a string of sweet text messages means they'll stay in touch.

For now, it's nearly Christmas, and Jamie has other worries. Like hitching a ride with his sister for the final leg of the journey. Like his car, stranded at the repair shop for want of parts. Like meeting his father's closest friend, Victor Leone, a stranger Jamie doesn't remember at all.

But when Jamie crosses his parents' threshold, Victor is no stranger. And even worse than the mutual shock of realizing he slept with his dad's best friend: Jamie can't stop craving an encore. It doesn't matter how powerfully the attraction simmers between them. If anyone learns the truth, their secret will ruin more than just Christmas.

Jamie knows Victor is off limits. If only he could make his stubborn heart believe it.

HEARTS RIGHT HERE

From road trips to isolated cabins, business partners to longtime besties, old crushes to new revelations, former bosses to dad's best friend... Delve into nine contemporary romances where friendship changes course.

Collection includes: Something Softer—Wishful Thinking—Very Close and All at Once—Just About Perfect—Running Hot—Anticipation—Matters of Heart—Right Here with Me—Put It in Writing

ASHES ON A DISTANT WIND

Before the Vrete came to Earth, Donovan Riggs was a man of faith. Now they're gone, and he's left that part of himself behind for good. In the ruinous aftermath of a war nobody won, he is simply trying to survive. With Beau Greer—a young medic who stumbled into his life and then refused to leave—Riggs travels dangerous roads between long-dead cities. Scavenging doesn't offer much of a future. It barely provides for the present. But Riggs will do anything to protect what's his.

EVERY SECOND YOU'RE ALIVE

Major Franklin Cade has spent years fighting the undead scourge that drove humanity from Earth. Now victory is in sight, but it's come at immeasurable cost. He has sacrificed everything in the line of duty—even his own heart.

For six months Lieutenant Daniel Mendoza has been missing in action. Only stubbornness and a refusal to tarnish Mendoza's memory have kept Franklin alive since losing the man he wouldn't admit he loved.

When a perilous rescue needs volunteers, he returns to the canyon where Mendoza fell. He is not prepared for the hope that ignites as he follows a fading distress signal across infested terrain. In the shadow of a deadly countdown every second is precious, but Franklin refuses to lose Mendoza again.

OPEN SKIES

After seven years working as partners, Kai and Ilsa are the best professional finders in the business. There's nothing they can't track down, no matter how unfamiliar the star system or hazardous the path. When a new client insists on accompanying the search for his daughter, Ilsa and Kai reluctantly agree. How can they refuse when Eleazar Dantes is desperate enough to pay double their usual fee?

But a high-stakes investigation is no time for distractions. Even more troublesome, when Kai realizes his true feelings for Ilsa, his timing couldn't be worse. Never mind that she doesn't seem to reciprocate: heartbreak is the least of their problems as the trail they're following grows dangerous.

With every step forward, Kai and Ilsa are more certain they won't find Eleazar's missing daughter alive.

SIMPLE AFTER ALL

Noah Fiore, contracts attorney and dedicated curmudgeon, spends every Christmas with his family on the shore of Lake Superior. It's practically tradition for his sister to invite some lonely acquaintance along for the festivities.

But this year's guest is no pity case. Riley Coto is a friend, whose warmth and charm instantly win over the collective hearts of the Fiore family—all except Noah, who remains as dour and unapproachable as ever.

Riley finds himself inexplicably drawn to Noah. Something tells him there's more to the man than stubborn work ethic and bad attitude. With Christmas fast approaching, Riley is falling for Noah, and there's nothing simple about that.